THE LUNATICK

More adventures to come in

MY FATHER IS A POLICE DOG

Mystery Series

DL ROSENBLIT

Copyright © 2020 by Donald L. Rosenblit

All rights reserved. No part of this publication may be reproduced, distributed, or transmitted in any form or by any means, including photocopying, recording, or other electronic or mechanical methods, without the prior written permission of the publisher, except in the case of brief quotations embodied in critical reviews and certain other noncommercial uses permitted by copyright law. For permission requests, write to the author, addressed "Attention: Permissions at roddyweiler@gmail.com

Collywood Productions
241 South 6th Street, #308
Philadelphia, PA 19106

Ordering Information:
For details, contact roddyweiler@gmail.com

Print ISBN: 978-0-578-80408-8
eBook ISBN: 978-0-578-81327-1

Printed in the United States of America on SFI Certified paper.

First Edition

www.DLRosenblit.com

Dedicated to:
Beansy
Nibby
Dixie
Brandy

Acknowledgments:

Claire Evens & Jennifer Rees
Every author needs a good editor.
I had two of them.

Scott Rosenblit
My creative guru.

Daniel Dulitzky
He blasted the cover illustration out of the park.

Chris Majowicz
He pictured Collywood and brought it to life.

Robert Herskowitz
Hubert Schlosberg
Bernard Spain
They believed in me.

Contents

Collywood Tourist Guide	ix
The Wonder Pups	x
Chapter 1: Mayhem at the Museum	1
Chapter 2: The Weiler Pack	7
Chapter 3: Germaine Shepherd	13
Chapter 4: The Wonder Pups	19
Chapter 5: The Dog House	25
Chapter 6: Collywood PD HQ	31
Chapter 7: The War Room	37
Chapter 8: The Lair of the Godfather	45
Chapter 9: Scene of the Crime	51
Chapter 10: Fart Facts	57
Chapter 11: A Hospital Visit	61
Chapter 12: The Envelope	67
Chapter 13: Busting Into Jail	71
Chapter 14: The Warehouse Bust	79
Chapter 15: Holy Hound Dog	83
Chapter 16: Dog-gone	89
Chapter 17: The Devils Den	93
Chapter 18: Lost Dog	97
Chapter 19: Roddy's Nightmare	103
Chapter 20: Security	109
Chapter 21: Like Caged Animals	115

Chapter 22: Live or Die	121
Chapter 23: Putting the Squeeze on Al K. Bone	127
Chapter 24: Hypnotic Spell	131
Chapter 25: Symbols	139
Chapter 26: The Fountain of Youth	145
Chapter 27: Failed Test	149
Chapter 28: Kick Tick Butt	155
Chapter 29: The Press Conference	159
Chapter 30: The Cure All	165
Epilogue	169
Chapter 1: Visitors from Pluto	171
Authors Note	173
About the Author	174

Collywood Tourist Guide

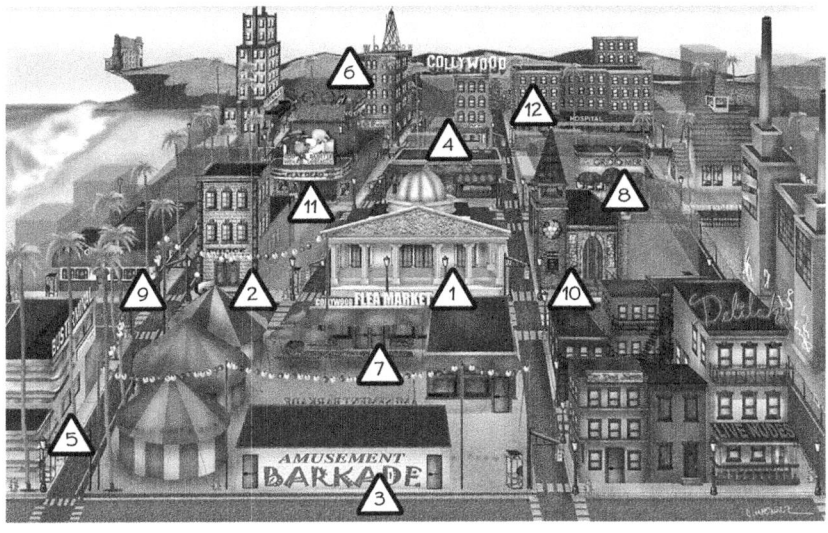

1 Collywood City Hall
2 Collywood PD
3 Barkade
4 Daily Barker Newspaper
5 Greyhound Bus Terminal
6 WOOF Broadcasting Company
7 Flea Market
8 Pierre Grooming Salon
9 Bone Giorno's Restaurant
10 Catholick Church
11 Collywood Movie Theater
12 Vets Hospital

The Wonder Pups

Cujo   Brittany   Roddy

Whinestein   Boomer

Chapter 1

Mayhem at the Museum

The Petropolitan Museum of Art stood majestically over the sprawling urban landscape. The city twinkled in oddly shaped patterns. Lines of tiny red lights crawled out of the city like obedient ants returning to their queen. The lively music and laughter of celebrating party animals crept up the hillside, but was cut short by a grove of evergreens guarding Collywood's famed cultural icon. The museum visitors had long emptied out through the manicured gardens and winding, tree-laden road that led to town. An ominous stillness gripped the hills.

Inside the dimly lit museum halls, paintings of the old masters looked down on a room empty of admirers. Towering statues of stone-faced canine gods guarded the grand entrance leading to the main gallery: Zeus, Apollo, Poseidon, Ares, and Hades. But even the most powerful gods in canine mythology could only stand by and watch the events that were about to unfold.

The Lunatick

At night, the museum belonged to Ollie McNally and Spike Spitz. The two aging guard dogs, both ex-Collywood police officers, made their nightly rounds with a swagger that shouted, "Hey, we own this place." Despite a sagging belly that nearly scraped the floor and shoulders stooped by age, Ollie's talented nose was as sensitive as ever. In his early days, Ollie had the reputation as one of the best tracking dogs at Collywood PD. His partner, Spike, was a police dog who pounded the beat in just about every neighborhood in Collywood. His aching paws and extra pounds did not slow his keen mind.

For many years these two best friends had walked the hallways of the museum protecting valuable treasures from imaginary art thieves. Spending their nights surrounded by art treasures, free from the rush of daytime visitors, was a great gig for two retired police dogs.

For their nightly rounds, they always met at the hulking statues of the canine gods. Ollie, the joker of the two, always engaged in a one-sided conversation with the statues. Knowing that the imposing gods, frozen in stone, could never break free of their moorings, Ollie felt free to smack talk the gods with all-in-fun insults, abuse, and one-liners.

On this night, it was Zeus's turn.

"Good evening Mr. Zeus—you hard-nosed excuse for a pooch."

"Be careful, friend," Spike quipped. "That's a thunderbolt

he's holding." Ollie held up his paws and feigned fear from the paw of Zeus.

Continuing through the hallways to the museum's grand hall, the two resumed their general chatter, which rarely changed from night to night.

"Hey, Ollie how many years have we been walking these halls together?"

"Too many to count."

"And how many art thieves have we busted?" Ollie rubbed his chin and thought for a minute. Spike raised his voice, "Well, how many?"

Ollie started counting on his paw, "Let me see." There was a long pause.

"None!" Spike responded with a raucous belly laugh.

Spike's ears suddenly perked up. He held up a paw to silence Ollie. "Hey partner, did you hear something?"

Ollie listened intently. "Nothing—but my talent is in my nose, not my ears."

Spike perked up his ears a little higher. "I could have sworn I heard something… strange."

"The only strange thing around here is you, pal." Ollie playfully poked Spike on the shoulder. Their words echoed as they entered the grand hall, a large, ornate room containing the museum's most valuable paintings. A large, surrealistic painting by Salvador Collie dominated the room. A plate under the painting revealed the name: *Everlasting*. The painting hung on the far side of the hall, bathed in lights that caused its dizzying display of colors and shapes to seemingly leap off the canvas.

Ollie was strangely attracted to Salvador Collie's great masterpiece. Each night, when making their rounds, Ollie would pause by the painting. His head would remain motionless, but his eyes scanned every inch of the canvas as if he were memorizing every brush stroke. Spike often found it necessary to physically drag Ollie away from the painting in order to continue their rounds.

As a working-class breed, Ollie had a limited education, but, over the years walking the halls of the museum, he had developed a strong appreciation for the art treasures that surrounded him. He enjoyed all the museum's wonders, but his fascination with Salvador Collie's *Everlasting* bordered on obsession. Like most of the great surrealist painters, Collie had hoped that his unusual style would stir up feelings and create controversy. The surrealist movement grew out of symbolism influenced by the founder of psychoanalysis, Sic-em Freud. Ollie had spent hours in the museum's library trying to find the right words to describe his strong feelings for the painting. Its composition, the strange illusion of light, color, and movement, it all overwhelmed him.

"What is so fascinating about that painting?" Spike asked for the umpteenth time. Ollie, who had tried many times to explain his interest in the treasures around them, welcomed his question.

"It's well known that Salvador Collie was a little bit batty, but his talent made him a legend. He loved controversy, and they say paintings like this one contain hidden messages."

Spike had stared intently at the painting, tilting his head from side to side before stepping back to get a wider view.

"Sorry pal, all I see is a spattering of color of odd shapes."

"My dear friend, I suggest, while making your rounds, pause by the painting and take a few minutes to study the brush strokes, the complex shapes and colors."

Spike's eyes shifted to the nameplate under the painting.

"Does the title give you a hint about what secrets may be hidden in the painting?"

"*Everlasting?*" Ollie pondered as he absentmindedly stroked the hair on his chin. "I'm working on it."

As the two friends studied the painting, the lights in the museum suddenly flickered, casting an eerie pattern over the canvas. A minute later, the room went dark except for the light that spotlighted the painting.

A startled Spike said, "What the ... who's messing with the lights?" His words trailed off as the lights went back on.

Ollie was so completely focused on the painting that he did not notice the pained look on Spike's face. Spike shook his head from side to side, fighting to reject the bewildering thoughts that blurred his mind. Suddenly, he advanced toward Ollie in a zombie-like trance. He paused momentarily, then picked up a small, marble statue and held it tightly in his paw. Sensing danger, Ollie's attention shifted away from the painting. He gazed at Spike's glazed eyes and bared teeth. A cold chill ran down his spine.

Spike's head was spinning out of control. Wild, divergent thoughts flashed through his mind. *You're my best friend. I hate you, I hate you. I would take a beating for you. You are my enemy and I will destroy you. Stop! Stop! Kill, Kill.*

Ollie was frozen in fear, staring at the statue held threateningly in his friend's paw.

"What's up buddy? Why are you looking at me like that?" Ollie retreated backward, his eyes focused on Spike's oddly twisted face.

"Careful, that's a 3000-year-old statue of Anubis, the Egyptian god of..." he gulped, "...*the dead*." Ollie was in full-fledged panic. "Put it down! You crazy or something?" Spike stared at the statue, mesmerized by the strange animal head perched atop a human body. His eyes shifted back to Ollie. A stream of drool slipped down his jowl. He raised the statue high and crashed it down on Ollie's head.

Chapter 2

The Weiler Pack

Rays from the morning sun sliced through the window and danced around the glass-enclosed display case. Specks of light flickered from the shiny objects carefully arranged on rich velvet. Roddy Weiler shaded his eyes from the sun's reflection and observed the medals, ribbons, and citations that his mother Winnie had made into a shrine. It was a colorful reminder of his dad's celebrity. Red Weiler Sr was a hero and there were intriguing stories connected to each award, which he had heard many times from his proud mom, embellishing his father's adventures. His dad didn't dwell on his life as a police dog, and seemed a little embarrassed by the display.

Rod, however, never missed a chance to remind Roddy of the family legacy of working-class dogs that immigrated to Collywood early in the century. Through the years, the Weiler's were known for protecting property and canines. They had a reputation for high moral principles and toughness tempered with fairness that won them respect from friends and foes alike. Through the years, the Weiler clan served the Collywood community as enforcers of the law. Rod carried on the family tradition as a highly decorated police dog. There was no question that his son, Roddy, also had the cop gene.

Roddy couldn't help but feel proud of his father's distinguished career, but as a dad, well, that was another story. Growing up in Collywood, a city dominated by the film industry, Roddy's life was far from normal. He lived in a canine tinsel town where dogs arrived daily from all over, filled with dreams of stardom that were rarely realized.

Roddy's gaze shifted to his father's bronzed Frisbee with the printed caption,

'Rod Weiler, Collywood High's MVP—Most Valuable Pup.'

• • •

"Hey dad, nice catch," Roddy yelled across the yard. Roddy's mom, Winnie who was sitting on the porch reading her favorite crime novel, jumped up and shouted,

"Woo-hoo—not bad for an old dog." Rod pumped a paw in the air, and then flung the Frisbee back at Roddy. He raced for the soaring disk, but the wind caught it and it flew just out of his reach.

"Come on Roddy, move it. It was right there in your face."

How about a pat on the head for a nice try, dad?

It wasn't enough that Roddy was an excellent student and excelled in just about everything he tried. Roddy was a natural athlete, but his interests were not on the Frisbee field. It bothered Winnie, who was well aware of the edginess between father/son. She spoke up for Roddy.

"What is the big deal about playing varsity Frisbee? You should be proud of Roddy for everything else he's accomplished. You can't relive your frisbee glory days through your son." Rod was a demanding father who expected nothing but excellence from his young pup. Ever since he was paper trained, Winnie would go out of her way to reassure her son,

"Dealing with bad dogs every day is stressful and dangerous, and takes its toll even on a tough cop like your dad. But I can assure you, that he's very proud of his very precious son."

The framed quote sitting on Rod's desk in his basement office, probably best expressed his attitude towards Roddy.

'One who challenges you and holds you responsible, loves you more than somebody who watches you stay the same and settles for mediocrity.'

• • •

Roddy's dad started in law enforcement as a police recruit, then as a private detective, and then back to serving Collywood as a police detective. He likes to say that he's done it all. Rod Weiler cut an imposing figure with his strong, compact appearance and dark piercing eyes. The Weiler clan went back generations—rugged dogs with great intelligence and crime-fighting instincts. Rod was courageous and fearless to a fault, which sometimes landed him in great jeopardy. After surviving an injury chasing a car, the great, gutsy cop slowed down a step or two.

Then he met Winnie prancing around at the local dog park. He was smitten at first glance. She had a distinctive look: black with mahogany-colored markings and a mahogany dot above each eye that accented her soft, gentle brown eyes. Rod circled around Winnie trying to sniff her butt, but Winnie's quick moves left Rod with his tongue hanging out. Rod kept visiting the same dog park hoping to see Winnie again, now with a gentler approach in mind. After several park visits, Rod's doggedness prevailed. Rod and Winnie started hanging out together and soon the tough, fearless crime fighter was a family dog.

In fact, Rod and Winnie were the perfect match: she was pretty much a crime novel junkie, always had her nose in a book, and was naturally inquisitive about the criminal cases that Rod was working on. At first, Rod dodged any discussion about his work at Collywood PD, but soon found it oddly productive to talk through his cases with Winnie.

The fact that Roddy was the only pup in Winnie's litter was rare. Winnie was sure that Roddy would grow up to have the strength and smarts of a whole litter of pups. And, just like his parents, Roddy's ears would always perk up when the conversation turned to crime.

In appearance, little Roddy was the image of his dad, just in a smaller package. This latest version of the Weiler clan showed extraordinary intellect, resourcefulness, courage, and leadership. On the surface, Roddy appeared to be just another bright, likable puppy, but don't be fooled, this pup was a phenom.

Chapter 3

Germaine Shepherd

It wasn't often that Winnie had both of her boys at the dinner table at the same time. In Rod's line of work, you don't pack it in at five o'clock. When most families were getting ready for bed, Winnie was often reheating dinner for Rod. Winnie had long accepted that her life would be one of waiting and worrying for Rod to come home at night.

Tonight, though, Rod had his nose buried in a crime report while dabbing at his food. An exasperated Winnie cleared her throat.

"Rod, can you put that paper down so that we can enjoy dinner as a family?"

Rod mumbled, "Give me a minute." Winnie rolled her eyes and turned her attention to Roddy.

"Roddy, there's one more biscuit in your bowl."

"Mom, I already had two," Roddy said, realizing that leaving one of mom's famous biscuits untouched would be considered to be an act of betrayal. Winnie turned to Rod for help.

"Would you explain to Roddy that a growing pup needs to feed his tummy to keep his energy up?"

An oblivious Rod peered up from his paperwork and grunted, "Do your homework son." Winnie threw up her paws and gave her patented 'I-give-up look'.

"Dad, I got my finals back today—all A's." Moments passed—no response. He raised his voice a notch. "I said all A's."

"That's good," Rod said unemotionally.

The scene around the table was interrupted by a knock at the door. Winnie pushed her chair back and stood up.

"Who could that be?" Winnie left the room and soon returned with Germaine Shepherd, who had recently been promoted to the position of captain at Collywood PD. Her mild mannered, easy-going demeanor was disarming. Germaine, in fact, was a tough-as-nails, no-nonsense female police dog who could give any male dog on the force a run for his money. Crime fighting at Collywood PD had often been an exclusive boy's club. But Captain Shepherd took on the boys and proved she was a very capable crime fighter. Strong, intelligent, brave, and ambitious, Germaine Shepherd and Rod Weiler worked as a team to take on the underbelly of Collywood crime.

Germaine gave Roddy an affectionate pat on his head, "Hi Roddy. Still killing it at school?"

"All 'A's' in his finals," Winnie said proudly.

"All A's? Good work son," Rod said, like hearing it for the first time.

"Germaine," Winnie said, "looking good in that uniform. I didn't have a chance to congratulate you. My goodness, a police captain."

"Oh, please," Germaine said, brushing off the compliment. "Sorry to show up at dinnertime, but Rod and I have some business to discuss."

"I think that's our cue to leave," Winnie said as she grabbed a few dishes and headed for the kitchen.

"Nice to see you…CAPTAIN," Roddy said with a smile. Germaine gave Roddy a paws up as he left the room.

"Rod, last night there was a robbery and assault at the Petropolitan Museum. I know that you're tied up helping the New Yorkie police with the theft of art treasures from the Guggenhound Museum, but there could be a connection between the two."

"I did hear something on the police radio about a commotion at the Petropolitan, but nothing about an assault and robbery."

"Maybe it's just a coincidence Rod, but, last night's robbery also involved the theft of a valuable painting. One of the guards was seriously injured." Germaine opened a small notebook."His

The Lunatick

name is McNally—Ollie McNally, an ex-cop. He has a serious head injury—falls in and out of consciousness—has no memory of the assault."

"How about suspects?"

"When the police arrived, they reported that a second guard was found staggering around the museum completely bonkers." Checking her notebook again, "He's also ex-cop—Spike Spitz."

"Spike Spitz? When I was a rookie we walked a beat together," Rod said with concern in his voice.

"Sorry, but we have Spike Spitz dead-to-rights—weapon in hand, covered in blood."

Suddenly, popping her head out from the kitchen doorway, Winnie said,"OH NO, not Spike. He's such a lovely dog and one of Rod's early mentors."

"WINNIE!" Rod barked. Winnie ignored Rods sharp stare. "Spike would never do such a terrible thing."

Winnie held her ground for a few moments, then in a huff retreated back to the kitchen.

Unknown to Rod and Germaine, there was someone else listening to their conversation. Roddy crouched a little deeper into the shadows of the upstairs hallway.

"What about the weapon?" Rod asked.

"Yes, Ollie McNally was struck on the head with a marble statue." Germaine checked her notes once again. "It was the statue of an ancient Egyptian god—Anubis?"

Still hidden in the shadows, Roddy remembered from a book he read on Mythology

'Anubis, the god of the Underworld—the protector of the dead—the body of a human and the head of a Jackal.'

"It's hard to believe that Spike would harm his fellow guard and friend" Rod's thoughts drifted back to his rookie year and his close relationship with Spike.

"Spike's paw prints were all over the statue," Germaine said. "We tried to question him, but he was completely out of it. There was no way to get him to talk rationally. He's in a cell now—pacing back and forth, rambling away, drooling all over the place."

"Hard to ignore the pile of evidence pointing to Spike's guilt, but this is not the Spike that I know. Let's go easy on jumping to conclusions." There was a moment of silence as the wheels turned in Rod's head.

Rod asked, "Who called it in, Germaine?"

"Someone touched off the alarm at one of the emergency exits. Our police dogs were able to respond quickly. They searched the building and found Ollie McNally unconscious on the floor and Spike Spitz lurching through the hallways in a daze, still carrying that bloody statue in his paw. It took three big huskies to subdue him."

"Any other paintings missing?"

"The museum curators did an inventory check late last night. It appeared that a Salvador Collie painting was the only one they couldn't account for." There were a few more moments for reflection.

"Rod, where are you on the Guggenhound theft?"

"The New Yorkie police did a thorough investigation of art dealers, auction houses and art collectors, but got nowhere. Then a tip came in from a reliable source that put the blame for the theft on some shady Collywood characters. We investigated most of our local Collywood art dealers and consulted with Jack Russell, the curator from the Petropolitan Museum, but so far few clues."

"What about mob boss, Al K. Bone?" Germaine asked. "Any chance that he's involved in all of this?"

"We're working on that angle. That dirty dog has been using his ill-gotten fortune to worm himself into Collywood society. Putting on a respectable act, he has a lot of Collywood socialites fooled."

"Rod, I know that you've got a lot on your plate, but I need you to jump on the Petropolitan case too. That's an awful lot to take on, but..."

"Sign me up."

Roddy, tucked away on the upstairs landing murmured, "Me, too."

Chapter 4

The Wonder Pups

The next morning, Roddy slipped out of the back door and surveyed his family's backyard. His face lit up with pride when he focused on a doghouse in the far corner of the property. He had begged for his own hideaway, and his father had obliged by building him a fine doghouse. Roddy remembered fondly how his dad and mom threw a party for Roddy to celebrate his new doghouse. Pups from all over the neighborhood came to help Roddy celebrate. When his dad lifted Roddy high in the air and hugged him tightly, it was a special moment Roddy, one that he wished would happen more often.

From all appearances, it looked like any old doghouse, but only Roddy and his friends knew what secrets it held. When his father built the doghouse, he had no idea that it was located over the abandoned basement of a big old house. Roddy had discovered the concealed room while burying a bone. To claim his domain, Roddy had tacked signs at the entrance of the doghouse warning the outside world of the dangers of trespassing on his domain:

Danger, Genius at Work!

Beware, Mad Dog!

Enter at Own Risk!

Trespassers Will Be Put to Sleep!

Just like his doghouse, Roddy was normal pup on the surface, but underneath, he was full of secrets.

Since he was a very young pup, Roddy had shown an interest in the criminal cases his father brought home from work. Little did his parents know that Roddy's curiosity was more than just being inquisitive.

Roddy looked around to make sure that he wasn't being watched, then reached into his pocket and took out a miniature Doggie Talkie. He pushed a series of buttons and barked out, "The lab, now." The message flashed through the neighborhood to four secure phones. Roddy Weiler and his four remarkable friends shared one stupendous secret: they were a secret society of teenage pups, responsible for taking a big bite out of crime.

The first to respond to the call was Whinestein. Whinestein was a pup prodigy, born with a high-powered brain capable of solving the most intricate problems. Even before he was paper trained, the gifted pup started to show inherent intelligence that was way off the charts. Prodigies are generally defined by their puppyhood ability to perform at adult levels, but Whinestein's genius far surpassed that definition. There was one special area of brilliance where Whinestein excelled. The bookish-looking pup with the big round glasses and his collection of bow ties was a wiz of an inventor, creating the most sophisticated gadgets and complex systems to fight crime.

• • •

Roddy's second recruit had been Cujo. He had little trouble persuading the affable Cujo to join his team. Cujo had the ability to handle difficult or threatening situations. Roddy knew that Cujo was able to make quick judgments. His solutions to problems were more likely to be practical and pragmatic—call it gut instinct. This was particularly important when operating in the crime-ridden, bad dog neighborhoods of Collywood.

It wasn't that Cujo didn't believe in book smarts. He had some of the highest marks in his class, but as he would point out to his honor roll friends, "Street smarts beats book smarts, any day." Where he grew up, Cujo made it known that the average pup wouldn't last very long without street smarts.

When Roddy's call came in, Cujo was playing a schoolyard pick-up basketball game. He was guarding a large Doberman about twice his size who was constantly talking trash to Cujo. The speedy Doberman put a move on Cujo and cut for the basket. Cujo reacted quickly. He jumped in front of the big dude, ripped the ball out of his grasp, and took it the length of the court. As he went up for a dunk, his Doggie Talkie vibrated. Cujo slammed the ball into the net, held on to the rim with one paw, and grabbed his Doggie Talkie with the other.

• • •

With her snappy demeanor, Brittany Spaniel came across as cynical and resilient—smart and pragmatic and exceedingly tenacious. Her intensive martial arts training made her utterly fearless and unafraid to take on the biggest and meanest hound that would get in her way. Roddy noticed these qualities in Brittany ever since she was a small pup. He recognized her as a fighter who would never admit defeat. Despite her upbringing as a spoiled valley girl, Brittany had all the tools to fit into Roddy's band of remarkable pups. She was a spirited sleuth with the brains and a cuteness that easily disarmed her toughest adversaries.

Brittany was hanging out with her friends at Collywood's famous Barkade when a pack of rowdy pups bounded down the hall right into Brittany's path. One particularly obnoxious hound got into Brittany's space and started to hassle her. A big mistake. Brittany let out a menacing growl, leaped in the air and lashed out with a 360 roundhouse kick that passed an inch from his snout. The startled hound reeled back, tripped over his feet, and landed flat on his back.

"And wipe your snout. Drool is not cool, dude," Brittany's scathing attack left the poor pup's tongue hanging out and tail dragging. Her Doggie Talkie vibrated, spoiling the fun.

● ● ●

And then there was Boomer. Boomer had many faults, but he also had one remarkable sniffer allowing him to track down anyone or anything, even when clues were few.

Boomer did not like taking baths, but loved rolling in the mud under his favorite tree. His next favorite thing was dozing off anytime, anywhere. He was a lovable loaf who never met a meal that he didn't like. Boomer was pretty much a loner simply because he could clear a room in seconds with one of his legendary farts. Boomer always sat alone at the school lunch table, until that time that Roddy decided to join him. Roddy saw something in Boomer that he liked and when he asked Boomer to join his team, Boomer was ecstatic to finally have such popular friends.

Boomer was in the middle of his favorite pastime, sleeping peacefully under his favorite dogwood tree, while unconsciously brushing away an annoying fly. Every time the fly landed, Boomer's leg lashed out at the fly. The fly was persistent and

The Lunatick

a lot quicker than Boomer's leg, but Boomer refused to let the fly disturb his nap. The fly versus Boomer's leg duel went on for quite a long time until Boomer's Doggie Talkie went off. Boomer snorted and jumped up in a cloud of dust, ending the skirmish with the fly.

Chapter 5

The Dog House

One by one, Roddy's faithful pups slipped through a loose board in the fence that circled the Weiler yard. First to enter was Whinestein, his large round glasses slipping down his nose, followed by Cujo, who's brawny body squeezed through the fence.

"What's up, pup?" Cujo went through a routine of high fours with Roddy and Whinestein.

Whinestein shook the sting out of his paw and whined, "Can't you come up with a less physical greeting?"

"We got to toughen you up, whiz kid." Cujo responded.

Brittany Spaniel, who had just wiggled through the fence, came to Whinestein's defense.

"Hey, Whinestein, how about inventing a muzzle that permanently seals Cujo's chops?" It was obvious that the pups had fun ragging on each other.

"So why the urgent call? Are we busting bad dogs today?" Brittany emphasized her willingness to mix it up with a swift karate kick. Cujo jumped back in a defensive posture and made a peace sign.

"Try peace, not violence, girl," he said.

"Look who's advocating non-violence," Whinestein moaned as he continued to shake out his paw that took the brunt of Cujo's greeting.

Boomer was the last pup to show up, and he made his entrance with a loud grunt as he squeezed his round body through the slat in the fence.

"Boomer, if you don't cut down on the biscuits, we'll have to widen the opening in the fence," Brittany said with a chuckle.

Cujo held his nose with his big paws, hiding a smile and asked, "How come the dawg with the most talented sniffer in Collywood can't tell how badly he needs a bath?"

"Hey, Cujo," Boomer countered, "sniff my butt."

Cujo raised his snout to the sky, dramatically sniffed the air, and then collapsed to the ground gasping for air. The group burst out laughing. It was hard to imagine that this innocent-looking, fun-loving pack of pups could kick some serious tail.

The five pups filed into the doghouse. Rays of light filtered through cracks in the roof, casting a cool pattern on the suddenly serious group of pups. Roddy peered out of the opening of the doghouse then proclaimed, "Coast clear."

Whinestein took the cue and pulled a lever hidden in a side wall. A section of the floor slowly opened, revealing a narrow stairway. One by one, the group descended into a semi-dark room. A soft whirring sound signaled the closing of the door above. Roddy clapped his paws sharply and activated a series of lights that flooded the secret crime lab. The pups had gathered in this underground hideaway many times, but still were awed by the colorful images of pulsating data on computer screens and high-tech equipment streaming out beams of colored lights. The home that once occupied the space overhead had long been torn down, but the basement had been transformed into an impressive crime laboratory. Each pup had contributed to the finished product in his or her own way, but they all knew that the real credit went to Whinestein, the inventor of the most remarkable crime-fighting technology. Roddy saw the proud smile on Whinestein's face. He put his paw on Whinestein's shoulder and whispered, "You done good, pup". Roddy picked up a device that looked like a TV remote on steroids. The lights dimmed and a large screen dropped from the ceiling. Roddy pushed some buttons and an overhead satellite image of Collywood appeared on the screen, then zoomed down to the Collywood Hills and the Petropolitan Museum of Art.

"This could be our biggest case ever. There was a robbery at the Petropolitan Museum last night and one of the guard dogs had his head bashed in."

A buzz filled the room. Cujo stepped forward, "I heard that there are some bad dogs out there that snatch valuable art works from galleries and museums and then sell them to private collectors with deep pockets."

"Could be," Roddy answered, "but like there's a bizarre twist to this case". For the next hour, Roddy went over the details of the unusual set of events that happened at the museum. Roddy worked the remote in his paw and on another screen, a new image appeared that took the pups on a virtual tour through the museum.

"All the art was accounted for except for a missing Salvador Collie painting."

"Who's Salvador Collie?" Boomer asked. Count on Whinestein's brilliant mind to answer.

"Salvador Collie is a famous Spanish artist known for his controversial paintings that focus on the subconscious mind."

"Cool," The wide-eyed Boomer responded.

"The thief could have hidden at closing then made his move when he felt the coast was clear," Brittany speculated.

"Maybe so," Roddy continued. "The alarm was set off when the emergency door was opened. The police report shows that the emergency door had been left open." The room grew silent. Roddy looked around and visualized the fertile minds of his friends churning away.

"Hey Brit, hack into the museum's security system and see

if the video shows anything suspicious." Roddy thought for a moment, then continued, "And also do a search on Salvador Collie and his painting, *Everlasting*. Maybe it will give us some kind of a clue."

It started as a low rumble. They had heard it before and knew what was coming. They looked at Boomer and in unison cried out,

"Boomer!" It showed all over his face. The funny little smirk, the innocent wide eyes, the incessant tail wagging.

"Fart attack," Brittany coughed out.

"Hit the switch," Cujo wheezed. Whinestein flew across the room, but before he could hit the exhaust fan switch, Boomer's blast of toxic wind crept out along the floor and rose, silently engulfing the room. In a desperate attempt to escape the foul smelling onslaught, the pups scurried into the far corners of the room. The coughing and gasping finally subsided as the powerful exhaust fan did its job.

"Okay Boomer, what did you have for lunch? And wipe that smirk off your face," Roddy scolded.

Boomer answered sheepishly, "Hot dog."

"Just a hot dog?"

"Chili dog."

Cujo shouted out across the room, "Boomer, how could you? You know what happens when you eat chili dogs."

"How many, Boomer?" Brittany admonished.

He pondered the question and said softly, "One."

She narrowed her eyes and asked suspiciously, "How many?"

There was a long pause. Boomer wrinkled his brow.

"Two." There was a pause.

"Three."

The pups responded in unison, "Three!" Boomer lowered his head and frowned. When the laughter started, his frown turned into a smile.

Chapter 6

Collywood PD HQ

Rod wasted little time in getting his nose into the Petropolitan Museum heist while still investigating the robbery at the New Yorkie's Guggenhound Museum. After accepting the case, Rod spent the next few days digesting the details of the robbery and assault at the iconic museum in the Collywood Hills.

Rod Weiler and Captain Shepherd studied photographs and documents of both museum robberies on a large evidence board at the precinct. The room was the heart of Collywood PD's investigative team. Several large monitors were mounted above the post-it laden evidence board showing a video of the interior of the Petropolitan Museum. Another screen flashed the mug shots of known criminal suspects.

"Hold it there," Germaine pointed at a photo that appeared on the screen. "When a serious crime happens in this town, you can't rule out the Dogfather." The menacing face that appeared on the monitor had a large scar that ran from the corner of one eye down to his jaw. He had sharp spikes on his collar and a crooked fang that jutted out from his lower jaw. It was the face of the notorious Dogfather, Al K. Bone.

From his ill-gotten gains, mob boss Al K. Bone had built one of largest, most pretentious homes in Collywood Hills. In size, it rivaled the mansions of some of Collywood's most prominent film mongrels. With all of the wealth that he had accumulated, the one thing that Al K. Bone could not achieve was respectability. Years before, he decided that a path to becoming socially acceptable might be in his collection of fine art. He spent a fortune on acquiring art from around the world. He attended auctions and used his power and money to gain influence among the diamond-collar set. If the greedy mobster admired a special painting that he could not purchase, he reverted back to his criminal ways and somehow acquired it without permission of its owner.

It was suspected that hidden deep in the tunneled maze under his mansion was a vault that contained many ill-gotten treasures.

Bone's photo triggered a deep scowl on Rod's face. "I hate that dirty dog," Rod barked out. "If it weren't for Flea Bailey, his legal beagle, he'd be residing permanently in the state pen."

One of the detectives standing nearby observed Rod's slow burn.

"I hear Bone's doggie breath alone is strong enough to knock you over." He held his nose and staggered around the room. That drew a laugh from a few other detectives standing nearby. Rod's intimidating look sent the detective scurrying back to his desk.

You could trace Rod's disdain of Al K. Bone back to when Rod was just a pup. Rod's father had retired from Collywood PD and taken a job as a security guard at Bull Mastiffs' Squeaky Toy Company. Bull had defied the mob in a kickback scheme on a big government construction job and hired Rod's father as a security guard. In what became the most tragic day for the Weiler family, both Rod's father and Bull Mastiff were gunned down in a mob hit. Although it was never proven, there were rumors pointing to a young Al K. Bone as the hit dog. Bone rose through the ranks of the mob through violence and intimidation before finally taking over as top dog: the infamous Dogfather. Throughout the years, the mere mention of the Dogfather's name raised the hackles on Rod's neck.

"Is there any proof that he had something to with the robbery?" Germaine asked.

"Yeah," Rod said, "the fact that he stole art treasures before—and his ugly face."

"I remember," Germaine said. "A couple years back. There was a robbery—a private art collection worth a fortune."

Rod thought for a moment and said, "One of the paintings was found hidden away in Bone's mansion. Too bad the mangy mutt had papers that said that it was a legit purchase. Bull, I say."

The monitor on the screen scrolled down, showing Bone's yap sheet for assorted crimes—everything from dognapping to assault with a rolled-up newspaper.

"Hi Dad." Rod turned abruptly and saw Roddy sitting at his desk.

"Roddy, what are you doing here? And you know I don't like anyone hanging out at my desk." Roddy abruptly slipped off the chair and looked innocently at his father.

"Gee, Dad, I just stopped by to say hello. You haven't been home much lately. Hello, Captain Shepherd."

"Roddy, it's nice to see you," Captain Shepherd said in a friendly tone. "But it's not a good time. We're in the middle of an important investigation."

"The museum robbery?" Roddy asked.

"Grrr!" Rod showed his impatience with his son. Germaine took Roddy's paw and started to lead him to the door. Roddy pointed at the big screen with Al K. Bone's infamous mug shot.

"Dad, do you think that Mr. Bone stole the painting?" Rod scowled at Roddy.

"Not now, son, this is grown-up business." Germaine said, in her calming voice. "You're always welcome to visit us Roddy, but not today."

Germaine turned away. Roddy waved good-bye but stood at the door for a few moments. With Weinstein's newest camera invention tucked in his collar, Roddy snapped pictures of the evidence board.

Chapter 7

The War Room

Finals taken—no more school until the fall. Lots of time to concentrate on solving crimes.

Early the next morning back in the crime lab, Brittany, Cujo, Boomer, and Whinestein watched as Roddy showed a hacked police video of the museum the night of the theft.

Brittany said, "The culprit must have entered through the emergency door by the grand hall. Someone had to have opened the door from the inside, but there is no evidence that anyone else was in the museum besides the two guards."

Cujo added, "Except for some stone-faced dudes lining the hallway." Roddy reversed the video back to the main gallery guarded by statues of Greek gods.

"The statues are Greek gods," Whinestein said. "There's Zeus, Apollo, Poseidon, Ares, and Hades, the most powerful canine gods in canine mythology. They lived and held court on Mount Olympus. The top dog of all the Olympian gods is Zeus, the protector and ruler of all canines. His weapon is a thunderbolt, which he hurls at those who displease him."

"Hey, Whinestein," Cujo quipped, "could you harness one of those bolts to put into our arsenal?"

"I would like to point out that there are also goddesses," Brittany said. "Like Athena, my favorite, who is the goddess of reason, intelligence, arts, and literature, but also fierce and brave in battle. Like me." Brittany emphasized her comment with a karate kick.

"Excuse me, history buffs," Roddy interrupted, "but we're in the middle of an investigation." He clicked on the menacing face of Al K. Bone. "Collywood PD suspects mob boss Al K. Bone in the museum theft."

"Al K. Bone is one scary-looking SOB." Whinestein said.

"Thanks to Whinestein's hidden camera tucked away in my collar, I was able to capture photos of the evidence board." Whinestein proudly gave it a paws up.

Study it carefully." Roddy continued. "There's probably some info that would give us a head start in solving this crime.

Brittany asked, "And why would someone go to all that trouble to steal just that one painting? There's so much amazing art in the museum and probably a lot that are more valuable."

"Everything about this case is puzzling," Roddy said. "I think you're right, Brittany. What kind of thief leaves behind valuable art and just takes one painting? They've got to be interested in more than just putting more biscuits in their pockets."

"Then what? And why?" a puzzled Cujo asked.

"Why that particular painting? Why did the guard get his head bashed by his friend?" Roddy shrugged his shoulders. "There must be something of value in the painting itself that would cause someone to go to so much trouble to steal it."

"From what I learned in art class," Whinestein said, "Salvador Collie was quirky enough to add something mysterious to his paintings. Some hidden message, maybe?"

"Whoa, that's weird," Brittany paused, then asked Roddy. "Anything else on PD's evidence board that caught your attention?"

"Thanks to Whinestein's miniature camera, we now have more information on the case, but there's still much to sort out." Roddy pointed to Whinestein and acknowledged his genius invention. A big grin spread over Whinestein's face. He put his paws together and applauded himself.

Roddy continued, "As you can see, the museum security cameras failed to pick up an intruder. They did capture Spike's attack on Ollie McNally and did show him taking the painting off the wall. Watch how the cameras caught him, staggering down the hall and handing off the painting to someone at the emergency exit.

"Seems that the guard just lost it," Cujo said. "But what caused him to go bonkers like that?"

"My dad partnered up with Spike when he was a rookie," Roddy said, "and he can't believe that Spike would attack his best friend." Roddy reflected for a few moments. "But the cameras clearly show that Spike and Ollie were alone in the museum that night."

The room grew silent, until Boomer blurted out, "Hey, let's get moving. What do you say, top dog, you got assignments for us?"

"We have lots of work to do," Roddy answered. Brittany took Boomer's paw, walked him over to a computer with a large monitor, and started punching keys.

Turning to Cujo, Roddy said, "Every visitor that walks in the door of the museum is photographed. You shouldn't have too much trouble hacking into the system to see if there's anyone or anything that looks suspicious."

"You got it. Using Whinestein's facial-identification software, we should be able to determine if there's anyone with a criminal record."

Whinestein tapped Roddy on the shoulder and asked, "How about me? What's my assignment?"

"I believe that you have a unique invention," Roddy said. "Now, it's just a hunch, but I would like to know if your invention could sniff out and identify any trace … ," Roddy cleared his throat, " … of poop?"

"Hey pup, what's poop got to do with it?" Cujo started to chant repetitively. "What's poop got to do with it? What's poop got to do with it?" Brittany joined in, "Yeah, what's poop got to do with it?"

Soon, all the pups started rapping, between laughs. "What's poop got to do with it? What's poop got to do with it?" They danced around until they dropped to the floor, giggling and panting from exhaustion.

"A fine bunch of crime fighters I have here," Roddy said with a chuckle. "Okay, let's check out your toys, Whinestein."

As Whinestein led Roddy to a door at the far end of the lab, he said sternly, "They're not toys, Roddy".

"I take it back, sorry."

The sign that hung over the door read *Whinestein's Workshop*. He punched in some numbers and opened the door. Then he activated a mechanism that parted the wall, revealing an array of impressive-looking devices.

"You are truly the Gadget King."

Whinestein, who delighted in praise, smiled as he took a long narrow cylinder off the wall. It had two holes in the end, looking oddly like nostrils. Whinestein often applied whimsical additions into many of his inventions. "Behold the *Super Pooper Snooper*," Whinestein said triumphantly. "Able to sniff out the most minute trace of poop." Roddy took the unusual device in his paws, gave a thumbs-up, and handed it back to Whinestein.

The Lunatick

"A demonstration my friends," Whinestein said proudly. "Boomer, would you please turn around and face the wall." The only movement from Boomer was a shrug of his shoulders.

"Turn around, Boomer," Brittany demanded. Boomer spun around to face the wall. Whinestein pointed the *Super Pooper Snooper* at Boomer, "Now raise your tail…a little higher—" Whinestein pushed a series of buttons and a load whirring sound filled the room along with lots of laughter.

"Boomer, about your butthole!" Cujo could hardly get the words out.

"Hold on a minute," Whinestein said as he reached for another device that looked like a big, fat writing pen.

Boomer spun around, "Don't point that thing at me." There was more laughter with a few snorts thrown in from these fun-loving pups.

"It's my newest invention, and maybe this is a good time to try it out." Whinestein handed the devise to Roddy. "See that button, click it once to start it up." Roddy obliged as a soft whirring sound is heard.

"Now click it twice." Roddy clicked it twice and a high-intensity light stretched across the room.

"Pretty powerful beam. So what happens when I click it three times?"

"You'll see," Whinestein cautiously backed away from Roddy and said, "go for three clicks, but concentrate."

Roddy held the devise gingerly in his paw. He clicked it three times, and suddenly a long flexible wand snaked out from the tip and danced around wildly around the room. Whinestein shouted out instructions as Roddy tried to tame the dancing wand.

"Listen carefully," Whinestein cautioned. "The wand has special sensors that read your slightest body and eye movements. It translates these markers and moves wherever you will it to go." Roddy's eyes widened in amazement.

"Don't grip it too tight and concentrate," Before long, Roddy's exceptional paw-eye coordination had the wand responding to his silent commands. Roddy joyously took the wand on its maiden voyage, darting into corners, under cabinets, and up to the ceiling, its high-intensity beam exploring every inch of Whinestein's Workshop. He then aimed the wand at the feet of his friends causing a 30 second dance recital. A wide-eyed Brittany said, "That-is-awesome. How can that long wand fit into what looks like a big fat writing pen?"

"I'm glad you asked," Whinestein beamed.

"As you noticed the wand that wanders out of the devise is actually a very thin wire made of tungsten the toughest metal there is. Besides tungsten's superior strength, I have added an element to the tungsten that makes the wand extremely flexible."

"Cool, what do you call this thing?" Roddy asked.

Whinestein responded dramatically, "*Wandering Wand*."

Chapter 8

The Lair of the Godfather

When Whinestein was greeted by the hostess at Bone Giorno's—one of Collywood's swankiest restaurants, he asked to use the restroom. The snooty hostess suggested that he use the big tree in front of the building.

"Rude," he said as he hurried past the hostess towards the sign that read *Restrooms*. Whinestein had printed out the restaurant's floor plan and knew exactly where to go. Dodging a few harried waiters, he went straight to an unmarked door, looked around, and cracked it open. Whinestein reached inside the door of Bone's empty office and planted a super-sensitive, miniature video camera next to the doorframe, then headed out of the restaurant.

Later in the day, Rod and Germaine walked through the door of Bone Giorno's. Tuxedo-clad waiters scurried around getting ready for the dinner crowd. The white-cloth tables were set with fine silverware and china. Attractive dogwood flower arrangements adorned the tables. It was an open secret that mob boss Al K. Bone ran his criminal empire from a back office at Bone Giorno's. There was no proof that Al K. Bone was involved in the Petropolitan or the New Yorkie museum robberies, but Rod delighted in hassling the mob boss every chance he could. A hostess with a menu in hand approached.

"Table for two?"

Rod flashed his badge. "I'm looking for Al K. Bone."

"Sorry, is he a patron?"

"Cut the crap, just tell him that Detective Rod Weiler and Captain Shepherd are here."

The flustered hostess scurried to the rear of the restaurant and disappeared behind a curtain. Germaine picked up a menu and checked the prices. She shook her head and said, "A little too rich on my salary."

A large, menacing pit bull lumbered through the curtain. His bulky figure almost filled the doorframe. He gestured for Rod and Germaine to follow. The pit bull tapped twice on a door, then opened it and gestured that they should enter. The room was dimly lit by an overhead light fixture, with little furniture except for some straight-back chairs around a cluttered wooden desk. Bone sat in a swivel chair that was turned toward the wall. He talked quietly into a phone. A few moments passed before he hung up and turned around to face his guests.

Bone's eyes were tired and glassy, and his balding head had patches of dirty grey hair over his ears. His jagged fang, jutting out from his lower jaw, glistened from the light above the desk. A sliver of drool ran down from his blubbery jowls. Rod's eyes focused on a diamond-encrusted dog tag that hung from his neck and felt a sharp urge to twist it around his neck. A large bowl of kibble sat on his desk. Bone ripped off the napkin that was tucked in his loud shirt, burped, then swiped his mouth with his sleeve. The gravel-voiced Dogfather spoke.

"Look, one more time, I know nothing about the heist of those paintings from the Guggenhound Museum in New Yorkie. You interrogated me and my associates numerous times and came up empty on any connection that I had with that robbery."

"Yeah, sure," Rod said sarcastically. "Not so empty as you might think, pal."

"Mr. Bone," Germaine asked, "can you tell us where you were last Wednesday night between the hours of ten and two PM?"

" What's this, something else that you're trying to pin on me?" A few moments passed Germaine noticed Bone fidget in his chair. "Wednesday night?" Bone scratched his chin. "Sleeping like a baby in my bed."

"Is there someone that can verify that?" Germaine asked.

"Sure, the sleep fairy. What—you don't believe in the tooth fairy?"

"Cut the BS," Rod said.

"Mr. Bone," Germaine said sternly, "is there anyone that can verify your whereabouts last Wednesday night?"

"Let me see…my bodyguard?"

"You mean your muscle-headed pit bull?" Rod said with contempt.

"Yes, I see you've met Brad Pit Bull. Brad, will you attest that I was tucked away in my bed last Wednesday night? Oh, wait, now I know what you're up to— you're grilling me because of the theft of that painting at the Petropolitan." Bone jumped out of his chair, pointed his paw at Rod and barked out.

"I had nothing to do with that theft or the one in New Yorkie. Now get off my back!" Rod stared down Bone and said, "Great…now we can cross you off of our suspect list."

"Mr. Bone," Germaine, playing good cop, said pleasantly, "we understand that you have an impressive art collection in your home. Do you think that you could give us a tour of your art treasures?"

"I think not. I'm particular about who I invite to my home. And I don't plan to put you on my guest list anytime soon."

Rod's scowl showed his contempt for Bone. "So, Mister Art Expert, you think all those pretty pictures makes you out to be some kind of a socialite? You're not fooling anyone.

You're still rotten to the bone; born in the gutter and you'll never leave it."

A furious Bone lashed out at Rod. "For years you have been trying to nail me for every two-bit crime that goes down in Collywood. But I'm still around, pal, with more scratch than you'll see in a lifetime." Rod and Bone were nose-to-nose, nostrils flaring. They glared at each other for a long moment. Brad Pit Bull, who was stationed at the door, moved toward the pair, but Germaine acted first and edged her way between the two snarling enemies.

"Okay boys, calm down."

Bone finally backed off and broke the tension with a hearty laugh.

"Mr. Bone," Germaine said in a calm voice, "your reputation leads us to question how much of this art was legally acquired. That, sir, makes you a suspect."

"Well, lucky me," Bone said sarcastically.

"One of these days your luck will run out," Rod said, getting into Bone's face again. "And I doubt if any of these pretty paintings will be hanging in your cell." Rod pushed the Brad Pit Bull aside and stormed out of Bone's office.

Chapter 9

Scene of the Crime

Later that evening, Roddy met up with Whinestein at the Petropolitan Museum.

"The museum is closed today," the burly police dog barked out.

Roddy glanced at his name badge and said confidently, "Officer Schnauzer, I'm sure you know my father, Detective Weiler?"

Officer Schnauzer's manner softened when he heard Rod Weiler's name.

"He asked me to bring him these papers." Roddy patted his pocket, giving the impression that there were papers inside his coat.

Officer Schnauzer looked at Roddy suspiciously. He held out his paw and said, "I'll see that he gets them."

Roddy pretended to contemplate the offer and then shook

his head, "He told me to personally hand them to him, sir. Come on, Officer Schnauzer, we'll be in and out before you know it."

The officer weighed the alternatives and said grudgingly, "Since you're Weiler's pup, I guess it will be okay. But don't be getting me into trouble now."

"Thank you, sir," Roddy said, rushing past Officer Schnauzer with Whinestein in tow. Unknown to Officer Schnauzer, Rod and the other police dogs had returned to headquarters and the two pups had the run of the museum. Before they left the crime lab, Cujo was able to shut down the museum's video system, so the pups felt free to roam without being discovered. Yellow crime scene tape marked a path directly past the canine gods guarding the entrance to the grand gallery.

Roddy stopped and addressed the Zeus statue. "We could get to the bottom of this mystery real fast if you could only yap." The stone-faced Zeus remained motionless.

Whinestein hiked up his glasses and said, "Oh great Zeus, father of all canine gods, god of the sky and lightning use your power to help us solve this crime." The two pups stood for a moment looking up at the statue's unseeing eyes.

Roddy broke the silence. "Guess sucking up to Zeus won't get us anywhere. We'll have to solve this case without the help of the gods."

Roddy pulled out a print of the museum's floor plan and led Whinestein on a roundabout route to the grand gallery.

Patting Whinestein's backpack, Roddy said, "Time to activate the *Super Pooper Snooper.*"

Whinestein nodded and pulled the odd device from his pack. He clicked on a switch and a small screen on the *Super Pooper Snooper* lit up, triggering a soft whirring sound. The young pups moved slowly down the hallway, eyes glued to the small screen. As they passed an emergency exit, the *Super Pooper Snooper* started to beep, slowly at first, then, as they moved down the hall, the beat increased.

"What's it telling us?" Roddy asked.

"Nothing yet," Whinestein replied as he pushed buttons rapidly. As they approached the grand gallery, Roddy held Whinestein back as he peered into the gallery that held the works of Salvador Collie.

"All clear. Let's get to work."

The two friends circled the room, Whinestein working his *Super Pooper Snooper* and. They moved cautiously, examining every inch of the floor. With tweezers and poop bags, they stopped every few feet to scoop up potential evidence. The two finally met at the faded patch of wall where Salvador Collie's painting had hung. The small, framed wall plaque was all that remained. Roddy studied it.

"*Everlasting,*" he repeated the name several times. Roddy stared at the space once occupied by the painting. The *Super Pooper Snooper* broke the silence with a whirring metallic sound.

Whinestein looked intently at the screen now spilling out data on its monitor.

Whinestein's eyes widened as he stared at the information. "Wait, this is strange."

"Hey pooch, something bugging you?"

"The read-out has identified an unknown insect species." Roddy looked over Whinestein's shoulder and studied the data on the screen.

"The *Super Pooper Snooper* is extremely accurate," Weinstein said. "Considering that there could be as many as ten million different kinds of insects in the soil beneath our feet, in the air above our heads, on all plants and animals, my device is pretty amazing, But, there's no way that I can explain this DNA reading," Whinestein shook his head from side to side. "I do believe that the poop identified indicates the subject could be an arachnid." The whirling sound of Whinestein's *Super Pooper Snooper* once more got Whinestein's attention.

"Okay, more information." With his face showing complete bewilderment, "The reading tells me that the subject has the DNA of several different species of the arachnid family, and that's impossible."

"Huh?"

"Yes, as strange as it seems, it's like someone put the DNA of a spider, a scorpion, and a tick in a blender and poof, you end up with one crazy, mixed-up arachnid. Except science doesn't work that way."

The two pups stared at the monitor of the *Super Pooper Snooper* and contemplated the consequences of Whinestein's discovery.

"Refresh my memory," Roddy said. "If I met a crawly thing walking down the street, how could I tell if it was an arachnid?"

"Basically arachnids don't have antennae or wings and they have eight legs."

"You know, I never stopped to count."

"Haha—funny."

"So, we have a possible suspect that doesn't really exist?" Roddy pointed at Whinestein's invention. "When's the last time you had that thing serviced?"

"That *thing*," clutching the *Super Pooper Snooper* to his chest, "is a highly technical wonder that can produce a DNA reading of any living organism in minutes."

"Except, your wonder left me wondering, who pooped on the floor?"

"I admit it is baffling," Whinestein said, checking the monitor once again. "This doesn't happen in the natural world." Silence filled the room as the two pups contemplated their discovery.

"It appears," Whinestein said, "what we have not one, but two mysteries to solve."

"Then again," Roddy said, "there's no evidence that our little whatever-it-is had anything to do with the events that took place that night." The two pups faced each other with puzzled looks.

Roddy continued. "Let's review what we know so far: Two guard dogs, Ollie and Spike. The best of friends, really close, like from the same litter. Spike suddenly goes berserk and conks Buster on the head with a marble statue."

Whinestein interrupted, "With a statue that just happens to be the Egyptian god of…" he gulped, "…death."

Roddy continued, "So, with Ollie unconscious on the floor, Spike takes down the painting, staggers down the hall to the emergency exit where he hands it off to an accomplice."

"So, if we let our imaginations run wild," Whinestein said, "perhaps our little creature jumps Spike and injects him with a venom so powerful that it produces a mind-altering meltdown."

"Where are you pups?" The angry voice of Officer Schnauzer reverberated down the hall.

"Guess the museum tour is over," Roddy said. They quickly gathered up their gear. Roddy took one last look at the empty space that once displayed the controversial Collie painting and ran out of the grand gallery.

Chapter 10

Fart Facts

While Roddy and Whinestein were tracking down clues at the museum, Brittany and Boomer huddled in front of a computer screen taking a virtual tour of Vets Hospital. Boomer kept his distance from the screen. Brittany motioned to him to come closer, but Boomer shook his head no.

"Germs."

"Our computers are pretty powerful," Brittany smiled. "But I don't think they're able to transmit germs." She reached out and pulled Boomer closer to the screen. "For someone who wallows in mud most of the time and hardly ever bathes, I don't understand your fear of germs." Brittany patted Boomer's sweater and a spray of dust escaped into the air. Brittany let out a fake cough.

The computer revealed page after page of data. Brittany paused at an article from the *Daily Barker* and read it out loud.

"From a small clinic that was founded to provide health services for the newly arrived settlers, Vets Hospital has grown over the years into a top medical facility. The hospital has an excellent reputation in the patient-care and medical-research categories and attracts top docs from all over." Brittany scanned further down on the screen. "The hospital was on the cutting edge in finding a cure for …" She couldn't help but giggle, "chronic flatulence."

Boomer's eyes lit up. "They found a cure for farting?"

Brittany continued, half reading, half laughing. "They recruited a group of acute farters."

"Cute farters?

"No Boomer ACUTE farters…like severe or extreme farters. Although, I most admit, as far as farters go, you're pretty darn cute." A smile lit up Boomers face as Brittany continued.

"The patients were fed large quantities of biscuits made from cabbage, beans, asparagus, cheese, and milk. Somehow, the test went south and produced a high level of noxious gas that spread to the entire floor of the hospital." She could hardly keep from breaking up. "The entire wing of the hospital had to be evacuated." She could read no further and doubled over in laughter.

"Sounds like my kind of test," Boomer said with a straight face. Brittany had to take a deep breath before continuing.

"Okay Boomer, here's a fart fact for you. A fart travels about ten feet per second. And the average dog farts fourteen times per day."

Boomer began counting on his paws. He counts and counts before saying, "Guess I'm not average."

"Far from it." It took a while for Brittany to compose herself before she turned her attention back to the computer screen.

"After their fart failure fiasco, doctors turned their attention to researching the treatment of parasites. By studying the habits of the parasitic carriers, they were able to develop vaccines that greatly decreased the incidence of some nasty diseases. Tests were performed on fleas that carried tapeworms, mosquitoes that carried heart worm larvae, and ticks that spread illness."

Brittany glanced up from the computer screen and noticed Boomer scratching his over-stuffed body. "Boomer, pay attention and stop scratching." She continued reading. "There were extensive studies on ticks and other arachnids by the hospital's top scientists." Brittany paused and asked, "Boomer, do you know a disease that is spread by ticks?"

"Lyme disease," Boomer said proudly.

"Good boy, Boomer." Brittany continued reading. "While feeding off the blood of victims, ticks were transmitting Lyme disease, which plagued the population of Collywood in epidemic proportions. Doctors at Vets Hospital worked long and hard to study this insect in detail." Brittany noticed Boomer's discomfort.

"Boomer, ticks are a real problem for our kind. That's why it's important to understand what makes a tick…tick."

Boomer smiled and repeated, "tick…tick."

"So, pay attention." Brittany turned her attention back to the computer and continued to read the information on the screen.

"Ticks are often thought of as insects, but are actually arachnids similar to scorpions and spiders. Ticks are parasites that feed on the blood of their hosts," She looked at Boomer. "Yes, Boomer, you and I are hosts. They lay in wait for us on grasses and shrubs. When we brush by a plant, they…" Brittany suddenly lunges at Boomer… "they land on us." Boomer jumped about two feet off the floor.

Boomer grabs his chest. "My heart—my heart."

"Boomer, I didn't know that you could jump that high. Haha" Brittany shut down the computer and took Boomer by the paw.

"Ollie McNally, you're getting visitors today."

Chapter 11

A Hospital Visit

"Did I mention that I don't like hospitals?" Boomer asked as he reluctantly followed Brittany off the hospital elevator. Brittany ignored the comment, grabbed a paw-full of Boomer's coat, and dragged him along.

"Let's see… room 725 must be down the hall."

Boomer's sensitive nose immediately picked up on the antiseptic smells of the hospital and he let out a quiet gag. As they walked down the hall, Boomer did everything possible to avoid eye contact with the patients. But as they headed down the hall, his head automatically bobbed from side-to-side, sneaking glances at each open door.

Brittany recognized his discomfort and said sympathetically, "Boomer, it's okay. You got your puppy shots—you're not going to catch anything." Boomer nodded but held his breath as long as a possible. He heard a low moan coming from one of the rooms and turned his head. Suddenly, a speeding hound dog whizzed by in a wheelchair, almost knocking him down.

Boomer yelled after him, "Hey, buddy, this isn't the Greyhound Raceway, you know." The hound dog gave him the paw. They continued down the hall, glancing up at the numbers over the doors.

"There it is, room 725," Brittany said. She gave Boomer a reassuring look and was about to enter the room when a nurse came rushing out.

"Sorry," she said almost bumping into Brittany.

Brittany peeked at the nurse's name badge and cheerfully said, "How's Ollie… Lolly?"

Lolly was noticeably overworked and overtired.

"Sorry, are you related to the patient?"

Thinking fast, the two blurted out, "Niece … uhh, father … I mean nephew."

Lolly hesitated for a moment, "The head injury is causing him to act…let me say, maybe not of this planet."

"You mean that Ollie is off his trolley…Lolly?" Boomer smiled at his clever use of words.

"He moans a lot and his eyes are glazed over. When he does speak, it's in Spanish, so I don't understand a word he's saying. The doctor should be making his rounds soon, he can answer your questions." Lolly checked her watch and turned down the hall.

The pups entered the room and found Ollie conked out with a large bandage wrapped around his head.

"He's sleeping, let's go," Boomer said, starting for the door. Without taking her eyes away from Ollie, Brittany waved him back to the bedside. The two pups stood quietly until Boomer finally said softly,

"Mr. Ollie McNally, sir, time to wake up." There was no response. Boomer opened his mouth to speak again when Ollie suddenly bolted straight up in the bed and started to talk fast and furious in Spanish. The startled pups jumped back, almost knocking each other down.

"What's that about?" a surprised Boomer asked as he backed toward the door. Brittany stood her ground, sorting things out. Finally, she said to Ollie,

"Como se llama?" Ollie turned to Brittany and spoke slowly,

"Me llamo Salvador."

"You understand what he's saying?" Boomer asked skeptically.

"Me duele la cabeza," Ollie continued.

"What did he say? What did he say?" Boomer asked as he returned to the bedside.

Brittany translated, "He said his head hurts."

Ollie turned cautiously on his side facing his visitors and moaned, "Tengo hemorrhoids."

"That's really more than I wanted to know," Brittany said.

Ollie suddenly reached up, grabbed Boomer's coat and pulled him closer. Ollie embarked on a barrage of incomprehensible sentences. Boomer put his paws over his ears in attempt to shut out the babble.

Brittany said, "It's Spanish. Ollie is speaking in Spanish." Ollie loosened his grip on Boomer's coat and Boomer jumped back out of reach.

A panting Boomer said, "He's an Irish Terrier, how come he's speaking Spanish? By the way, where did you learn to speak Spanish?"

"I'm good at languages, and I once had a boyfriend that was part Chihuahua. Poor Ollie… I once read that someone with a serious head injury could suddenly start talking in a language that they were not familiar with."

"Whoa."

"I would guess that he has no idea what happened at the museum. It seems that old Ollie believes that he's actually the artist, Salvador Collie."

"That's weird," Boomer said. "Did you catch anything else he said?"

"He was jabbering away so fast it was hard to understand him."

"What are you doing here," the booming voice in the doorway asked? Boomer's mouth opened, but no words came out. "I'm Dr. Hindlick, Ollie's doctor. I left instructions that he was not to be disturbed." Dr. Hindlick was dressed in green scrubs with a surgical mask dangling from his neck. Grey hair stuck out from a surgical cap perched on his head. Dr. Hindlick stared at them suspiciously and with a stern voice he repeated, "I said, what are you doing here?"

"He should work on his bedside manner," Brittany whispered to Boomer.

"Just checking on an old friend," Boomer shook Ollie's paw vigorously. "See you — bye." Boomer nudged Brittany toward the door. Dr. Hindlick stood his ground, blocking the entrance.

Suddenly, Boomer started to gag as he staggered toward Dr. Hindlick. It was part exaggeration, but the hospital setting, the smells, the stress all seemed to have caught up with Boomer and he let out one of his legendary farts.

A stunned Dr. Hindlick grabbed his nose and stepped aside as the two pups rushed out of the room. Boomer turned back to Ollie as they left the room. "Bye now Ollie, feel better."

Ollie propped himself up in the bed and pleasantly replied, "Muchas gracias."

Chapter 12

The Envelope

The miniature video camera that Whinestein attached to the doorway of Al K. Bone's headquarters, was programmed to record when a voice was detected. Roddy had been watching the video for over an hour and got a big dose of foul language and dishonest dealings. As he scanned through the video he witnessed the confrontation between Al K. Bone and his father with Captain Shepherd acting as referee. He was disappointed that so far the video did not reveal any further discussion concerning the Petropolitan Museum robbery and assault. Then Bone's phone rang.

"Bone here…so the goods will be delivered…when? Yeah, the warehouse…Next Tuesday… Around midnight. Be on guard…Valuable cargo." Roddy rewound the tape of Bone's phone call and watched it over and over again.

The words from the phone call rolled around in Roddy's

head. *Could the cargo be the stolen art treasures from New Yorkie? The call could be just about anything,* One thing he was sure of, he had to get this new information to his father. But how to do it without revealing the identity of the messenger would be tricky.

• • •

Roddy set his alarm to be the first one up the next morning. He was out the door even before the Daily Barker newspaper arrived. His dad's car was parked in the driveway and Roddy was hoping that the car wasn't locked. He squeezed the door handle and it opened. Roddy took an envelope out of his pocket and placed it on the drivers seat.

Back at the breakfast table, Roddy picked at his bowl of biscuits. He watched as Rod gobbled down his kibble. "Dad, could you drop me at City Hall on your way to work?"

Rod nodded 'yes' without missing a bite.

"My boys are up early this morning." Winnie appeared in the dinning room in colorful robe and in her funny doggie slippers. She threw a kiss Rod's way and patted Roddy's head. "Now that school is over, I thought you would be sleeping late."

"I'm meeting Cujo this morning at City Hall, then we're hanging out in town. Dad's dropping me off." Roddy took one more bite of his biscuit and headed for the door, where he turned and waved goodbye.

Roddy was in the passenger seat when Rod came out of the house. He watched as his father got into the car.

*Oh no…*Roddy face scrunched up, as the envelope slipped to the floor. The car pulled out of the driveway as Roddy was trying to figure out how to bring attention to the envelope.

"Dad—what's that…?" Rod glanced his way. On second thought, Roddy didn't want to appear too obvious and changed the subject. "So dad, what a coincidence that you're working on museum thefts in New Yorkie and here in Collywood." Roddy stiffened when he saw the scow on his dad's face.

"How do you know that, son?"

"Uh, mom told me."

"Roddy, this is serious police work. You have to keep your nose out of my business."

Roddy took a deep breath, "Okay dad, I've been wanting to talk to you about that. I'm a Weiler and I'm expected to follow in your footsteps and like all the Weiler's before you. I would like to get a head start in becoming a great police dog like you. Teach me, dad. I'm ready."

Rod absorbed Roddy's comment in silence. The car stopped in front of City Hall, but Roddy didn't move.

"You're right son, like all the Weiler's before you, your future as an enforcer of the law is pretty much in your future.

And I bet you'll be darn good at it. But, you still have some growing to do and I'm not sure that you're ready to deal with the crime-infested side of Collywood."

What a break through! Dad, finally talked to me about some serious stuff—my future. The high that Roddy was feeling suddenly took a tumble when he thought about the consequences that he would face, if his dad found out about his secret life. The deception in hiding the crime fighting activity of his Wonder Dogs, weighed heavily in Roddy's mind.

His dad continued."Yes, Roddy, I have been investigating a theft from the museum in New Yorkie, but I've yet to come up with solid evidence that would bring a close to the case. And I'm just beginning to wrap my head around the Petropolitan theft and assault.

"Thanks dad, for letting me on that information."

Roddy's eyes shifted to the envelope on the floor, *The envelope, the envelope on the floor by your foot. Pick it up. Pick it up.*

"But for now, that's all I'm ready to discuss with you." Rod leaned over and patted Roddy's paw.

"Be patient, Roddy. Be patient."

Chapter 13

Busting Into Jail

Roddy was sprawled out on the steps of the Collywood's majestic City Hall repeatedly glancing at the big clock located in the tower jutting into the sky.

City Hall is home to Collywood's government and the local jail and is Collywood's tallest building. The square design surrounds an interior courtyard, and it is topped by a bronze statue of Lassie Collie, Collywood's founder. The buildings exterior and interior sculptures were designed by the famous Chinese architect, Shar Pei. The buildings tower also featured large clocks on all four sides and an observation deck below the base of the statue that allows visitors to observe all of Collywood and its surroundings,

Roddy sat up abruptly as his Doggie Talkie vibrated."Cujo— where are you?"

"Be there in a sec."

Roddy had researched the layout of City Hall and pinpointed

the location of the jail cells. The mystery of the missing Salvador Collie painting was becoming more complex, and Roddy wanted to talk directly to Spike Spitz. Cujo turned the corner at full speed and raced toward Roddy.

"Gotta get back to the gym," Cujo panted as he dramatically patted his chest with his big paw. Roddy smiled, knowing that Cujo was in great condition and one of the fastest runners at school. Roddy and Cujo stood before the cascading steps that led up to the City Hall entrance.

Looking up at the barred windows on the upper floors, Roddy said,

"Let's get to work."

He took a jacket out of a case and handed it to Cujo who held it up and read the lettering across the front, "Roddy's Janitorial Service. Cool."

"Wait, there's more." Roddy pulled a scrub brush out of the case and handed it to Cujo. "You do the scrubbing." He then took out a mop and said, "I'll mop up after you. Haha"

The pair walked confidently into the building, past a guard completely absorbed in the Greyhound Racing results in the Daily Barker.

"Cleaning crew," Cujo said as they hurried into an open elevator. Before the guard could look up, Roddy had pushed the button labeled Corrections. The door closed and the elevator climbed slowly. As they watched the numbers flash by, Cujo asked, "You got a plan, boss?"

"When the door opens, you club the guard with the scrub brush, and I'll head for the cells."

Cujo's eyes widened, "You're pulling my leg, right?"

"All 4 of them."

Roddy smiled. The door opened and they were met by another guard, sitting behind a desk, chatting away on the phone. Cujo held up the scrub brush menacingly, then yanked it down as the guard glanced up. He was a tough old hound who looked at the pair suspiciously. Roddy pointed to the lettering on his jacket. Without waiting for the guard to respond, he pulled Cujo towards a door that read Cages.

"Just a minute there," the guard called out.

"Busted," Cujo said under his breath. The two stopped abruptly. Roddy turned to the guard with the mop partially concealing his face and waited for the worst.

"Here, you'll need these badges," the guard said. Roddy started breathing again and reached out for the badges. The guard eyed them warily and said,

"Starting them off pretty young nowadays."

Roddy dragged Cujo through the door as Cujo quipped, "Fortunately, not the smartest guard on the block." The pups stared down a long row of cells lining each side. Roddy dropped the mop head to the floor and swished it around aimlessly as the pair ambled down the corridor glancing into the cells. The heavy bars that separated the prisoners did little to put Roddy and Cujo at ease, although most of the detainees looked pretty tame. As they walked along, they were surprised how many of the cells were vacant.

Cujo joked, "Maybe they went out for a beer?"

"I doubt it, not when there's plenty of bars up here." Cujo's burst of laughter caused a stir among the prisoners. Roddy had to cup his paw over Cujo's mouth.

"Enough! This is serious stuff," Roddy said as he mopped his way past the cells. A mournful wail got their attention. They quickened their pace and finally reached the cell that was Spike's temporary home. Peering through the cell bars, they saw Spike curled up in a corner.

Roddy said softly, "Spike, Spike Spitz, can we talk to you?" Spike looked up slowly. His eyes darted around the cell and finally came to rest on the two pups.

Roddy continued, "We're gathering information on the museum investigation. Can you tell us what happened?"

"How is Ollie?" Spike asked in a surprisingly clear voice.

Roddy faked his response. "He's good. Feeling a lot better."

"They won't have to put him to sleep, will they?" Spike said, his voice cracking with concern.

Roddy and Cujo shook their heads and Cujo added, "No, nothing like that. He's doing fine. He'll be leaving the hospital any day now."

"I don't understand what happened," Spike said hesitantly, and then began to ramble on non-stop. "We were doing our rounds, yapping about our usual stuff, and suddenly, I just lost it, couldn't control myself. I heard a voice, it kept telling me to pick up that statue and ..." Spike's face scrunched up in pain. "That voice—it forced me to..." Spike's eyes watered up. "I love Ollie, how could I hurt him? Now, they've got me locked up for hurting Ollie. Please tell me it was just a bad dream?"

Roddy waited for Spike to calm down and asked, "Spike, think back to what happened right before you lost control." Spike blinked his eyes rapidly, trying to clear the fog from his head.

"We were standing in front of that painting that Ollie liked so much."

"Salvador Collie's Everlasting?" Spike nodded 'yes'.

"He was jabbering away about symbols and secret messages, and suddenly I felt like someone, something took control of my mind." As the memory of the awful event passed through his mind, Spike began to softly whine.

Roddy hesitated and then asked, "Just before you lost control, did anything unusual happen?"

Spike shook his head, trying to clear the cobwebs clouding his brain.

"Like some kind of a bite, maybe?" Roddy asked.

"I was wearing a flea collar." There was a long pause. Roddy saw Spike's eyes narrow in deep concentration. A light seemed to go off in his head and he said excitedly, "Yeah, I think so, right here on my neck." Spike put his paw up to his neck and pressed his head against the bars. Roddy reached in, separated the hair on the back of Spike's neck, and a grim look crossed his face.

"Whoa," Cujo's eyes widened. "Looks like something made a meal out of your neck." Looking at Roddy incredulously, he asked, "You know of any vampires sucking around Collywood?"

Roddy shook his head. "Actually," Roddy said in a somber voice. "I think we're dealing with another kind of bloodsucker."

● ● ●

The two pups sat on the steps of City Hall after their visit with Spike.

"One might think, like case closed." Cujo said. "Spike assaulted Ollie, then handed the painting over to a partner in crime. But Spike's story and that bite on his neck sure messes up that assumption."

"For now Collywood PD is laying the guilt on Spike for obvious reasons. My dad has known Spike since he was a rookie and believes that the whole story has yet to be told."

Whinestein's Super Pooper Snooper revealed that some unknown creature was able to inject Spike with a powerful mind-altering venom. As we just saw, it was with a bite to Spike's neck. That caused Spike to go batty, attack Ollie, then passed the Collie painting to someone at the emergency exit."

"Wow, that's a lot of trouble to go through just to steal a painting." Cujo said. "Especially a painting that doesn't touch the value of many other paintings in the museum."

"Just one of many questions that need answers," Roddy said. "Thanks to Whinestein's invention, we do know that this is no ordinary insect. From the poop droppings that were found at the museum, Whinestein's sleuthing found that it was some kind of an altered arachnid with the DNA of a spider, scorpion, and tick all in one creature."

Cujo cringed as an image crossed his mind. "A bloodsucker and poisonous like a scorpion. Ugh!"

Chapter 14

The Warehouse Bust

It was the same routine at the Weiler house on this Tuesday morning. Rod was gobbling down his kibble with his nose buried in the pages of the Daily Barker newspaper. Winnie made her entrance just as Rod pulled his chair away from the table. Winnie patted Roddy's head, but this time she gave Rod a big hug.

Roddy knew that tonight was the night that Al K. Bone was supposed to be receiving stolen goods—maybe from the New Yorkie museum theft. When he last checked, his dad had not discovered the envelope in the car, and Roddy was going bonkers.

"Dad, would it be okay if I hung out with you at HQ today—like we talked about?"

"Talked about what?" Winnie asked.

"Your son thinks he's grown up enough to start training to be a police officer."

"Not saying training as yet, I just want to be around you more at police headquarters."

"My little boy is much too young to think about gangsters and robbers and dognappers."

"First of all, your little boy is not so little anymore. I'm a Weiler; expected to be a cop so why not start to learn what policing is all about?"

Winnie was in deep thought and finally blurted out, "I was hoping that you might become a lawyer," and with her voice trailing off, "and not a police dog." There, she said it. Winnie wanted Roddy to be a lawyer and not a police dog. Rod said not a word and just walked out the door leaving Winnie to ponder just how Rod felt about his son, the lawyer.

H'mm…lawyer—police dog—lawyer—police dog. Roddy tossed it around in his mind.

Roddy followed his dad out of the door and watched as he opened the car door. Roddy had snuck out during the night and put the envelope back on the seat.

As Rod was about to jump into the car, he saw the envelope.

"Whoo hoo," Roddy said as his dad read the note. Rod slammed the door, gunned the car, pulled out of the driveway and sped down the street.

Wow, if I could help dad apprehend a criminal and bring him to justice in a court of law…hey, I sound just like a lawyer. A big smile lit up Roddy's face.

●●●

Rod hurried through Collywood PD HQ and tapped on Captain Shepherd's door before entering. The captain was talking on the phone. Roddy anxiously paced the floor waiting for the phone call to end. Germaine noticed Rod's impatience. She said a few more words, then hung up. "What's up?"

"Did you put a tap on Bone's phone?"

"We would need a court order to that. Why are you asking?"

Rod handed the note to Germaine. As she read the note, her tongue slipped out to one side of her mouth—a trait that Rod noticed about Germaine when caught by surprise.

"Where did you get this?"

"It was left on the seat of my car by someone who, obviously, wanted anonymity."

"How reliable can it be?"

Rod shrugged his shoulders. "It could be our first break in getting a handle on the New Yorkie stolen art." Germaine picked up the note again and read it out loud:

"Bone here…so the goods will be delivered when? Yeah, the warehouse… next Tuesday… around midnight. Be careful…valuable cargo."

Germaine opened her desk door and pulled out a file labeled '*Al K. Bone.*' As Rod looked on, she scanned through the pages. A few minutes went bye before Germaine spoke.

"If we pursue this tip, I see nothing in Bone's file that

would give us an idea of the location of a warehouse. And this meet-up is to take place tonight?" Rod nodded yes.

"Outside of a few high-level officers, who would even know about our involvement in the New Yorkie heist?"

"And who would know where you lived?"

Rod rubbed his chin as the wheels turned in his head. "Look...if anyone could pull off a theft from Guggenhound museum, it would be Bone, right?"

"Right! And if it turns out to be a phony lead...we could be in deep poo." There were a few more moments of reflection.

"I say, let's go for it." Germaine said emphatically. "And for all we know, we might also find a connection to the Petropolitan Museum assault and robbery."

"Right!" Rod said with a little less conviction. Two of Collywood PD's top police officers knew that the decision to raid the warehouse would be a risky one.

"So, where do we find this mysterious warehouse?" There was a long silence. Finally, Rod spoke,

"I've got a plan."

Chapter 15

Holy Hound Dog

Winnie used a dog whistle to summon Roddy when he was in his dog house. Whinestein had rigged a device that transferred the sound of the whistle to a speaker in the secret lab. Roddy was immersed in data from searching the Internet and found himself up to his ears trying to sort out the strange circumstances surrounding the Petropolitan Museum robbery and assault and helping his dad solve the New Yorkie Museum theft of art treasures.

Winnie's whistle blared over the speaker; Roddy climbed the stairs and was out in the yard in a minute.

"Roddy! Roddy!" Winnie yelled from across the yard. "You're on your own for dinner tonight. I have a PTA meeting and your father will be home very late. There's a can of liver in the fridge and some biscuits on the counter."

"Okay, mom." Roddy turned away from his mom— "LIVER!" He stuck his paw in his mouth and pretended to gag.

The Lunatick

So dad won't be home until late tonight—he's acting on my tip, If there's a reward, I should get some of it. Don't be greedy, Roddy—just hope he makes it home safe tonight.

• • •

At Rod's suggestion, Germaine put a tail on both Al K. Bone and his bodyguard, Brad Pit Bull. If the tipster was correct, one or both of them would lead the police to the warehouse. Waiting near the phone in Germaine's office, the clock on the wall read 9:20 PM. Midnight was the time that the delivery would be made, but the suspects could be on the move at anytime. Rod paced the floor as the clock ticked away at an unbearably slow pace.

"The squad car is waiting outside?"

"Yes, Rod."

"How many cops are standing by?"

"Altogether—10."

Rod stepped up his pacing.

• • •

Roddy was all nerves. He walked a circular path through the living room, dinning room and kitchen. Always stopping to look at the clock hanging over the sink. Roddy heard a key in the door—his mom arrived home from her PTA meeting. It's 11:15.

"You still up? Oh my, the meeting was so long. They're making some curriculum changes for the fall semester that I'm not really pleased with. But they did have a lovely assortment of biscuits." Winnie went on and on, but Roddy heard not one word. His mind was on an unknown destination in downtown Collywood. Winnie finally stopped talking and headed up the stairs. Roddy glanced at the clock.

Midnight!

It was close to 2:00 AM before Roddy fell into a restless sleep, full of wild dreams. The next morning he was at the breakfast table early. Winnie had mixed some fresh baked biscuits with the canned liver that Roddy left untouched the night before. A few nibbles were all he could stomach.

"Did dad leave for work already?"

"Still sleeping. He got home very late last night."

"Did he seem okay? He's been working very hard lately."

"Couldn't tell, I just rolled over and fell back to sleep."

Not knowing what happened at the warehouse was driving Roddy batty. He discretely questioned his mom, hoping his dad gave her some hint as to what happened the night before.

"Roddy, what goes with you? What is so important about last night? Are you all right?"

The Lunatick

No, I'm not all right! My head will explode if I don't find out what happened last night.

• • •

Back to the night before. It's 11:35PM. Still no word. Rod's thinking that the tip was bogus. That thought is wiped from his mind when the phone rings. Brad Pit Bull is on the move. The police follow at a discreet distance. The word from the police detail assigned to Al K. Bone reports that he has not left his mansion. Rod and Captain Shepherd jump in a squad car and take off. They soon catch up to the other squad cars tailing the suspect. The suspect's car soon reaches its destination; a warehouse on Turd Avenue. Brad Pit Bull gets out of his car and enters the warehouse. Rod eyes the exterior of the building, no signs identifying a company name. It's a dark, chilly night; raindrops dot the car's windshield. The street light in front of the building is busted, adding to the dreariness of the night. A truck turns on to Turd Avenue and blinks its lights 3 times. Several huskies appear and wave to the driver to back up to the loading dock.

"Wait until I give the word before moving in," Germaine orders over the police radio.

The truck's sliding door rolls up and the huskies join the truck driver in unloading 6 large cartons.

"GO!" Germaine barks out and ten police dogs swarm the warehouse.

"Down. Sit. Stay!" The officers shout out their commands. The startled huskies drop to the floor, except for Brad Pit Bull, who stands his ground.

"I know my rights. You just can't storm in here and order us around, We'll sue your tail off." Captain Shepherd takes a paper from her uniform pocket and shoves in Pit Bull's face.

"Here's your court order, now break open those cartons." Reluctantly, Pit Bull nods to several of the huskies, who pick up crow bars and crack open the cartons. Rod and Captain Shepherd stare at the goods laid out before them.

"Holy hound dog!"

Chapter 16

Dog-gone

"I got it," Winnie called as she greeted the phone caller in her usual cheerful style. Roddy hesitated at the door when he saw his mom's cheery face turn to concern.

"Rod," she called. Rod bounded down the stairs and entered the room. She put a paw over the phone and whispered, "It's Germaine. She sounds terribly upset." Rod took the phone. He listened intently for a few minutes, responding only with a few grunts.

"Okay, I'll see you there." Rod hung up the phone and turned to Winnie. "We got trouble."

"What happened?" Roddy asked from the doorway. Winnie's inquiring eyes asked the same question.

"Ollie is missing from his hospital room." His concern was reflected in his voice. Besides being a valuable witness to a crime, Rod had warm feelings for the two old police dogs that had served

Collywood community for many years. "One of the nurses found Ollie's bed empty. Someone must have grabbed him."

Winnie, always the optimist, said, "Poor Ollie. You said he was confused, maybe he wandered out of the hospital and got lost?"

"Don't think so," Rod said. "Not in his condition." Roddy pondered how much he should say about the investigation.

"If anyone can find Ollie, it's you, Dad." Roddy said while rushing out the door in the direction of his dog house.

• • •

Roddy descended the stairway leading to the secret lab and saw that his friends had already assembled. The powerful computers that Whinestein had assembled were being used to play computer games. The awesome graphics and effects displayed on a large monitor were better than any games that could be found at Collywood's popular Barkade.

"Direct hit!" Brittany cried out as Cujo's spaceship went down in flames. Boomer and Whinestein cheered as the vanquished Cujo crumpled to the floor, thrashing his legs in the air.

"I take it, Cujo lost?" Roddy asked.

Brittany said excitedly, "We're kicking Cujo's butt. Woohoo!"

Cujo groaned, "They ganged up on me just when I was fighting my way through a nuclear wasteland." It was unusual for Roddy to show such little emotion.

"You okay, Roddy," Brittany asked?

"Kind of been moping around lately." Boomer added.

"Yeh, what's going on dude?" Cujo said as he landed a soft punch to Roddy's shoulder.

"Nothing, really, I'm fine." Roddy said as he plopped down on a bean bag. The four friends were not buying it.

"Come on alpha dog" Brittany said, "What bugs you, bugs all of us." With that comment, the four friends jumped on the bean bag burying Roddy with flailing legs and legs. Laughing breaks out and doesn't stop until Roddy fesses up to what is bothering him.

"Okay, okay I'll tell you what's bugging me. I'm concerned about what I'm getting you guys into, with this really scary arachnid. You all know what a single bite from this devil can do to you." The fearless pups, well aware of the potential danger that they could be facing, would not let it get in the way of their bravado.

"Adding to this mystery, Ollie, the injured museum guard, is missing from his hospital room."

"No way" Britany exclaimed. "The Ollie McNally that we saw at the hospital, would in no way be able to take off on his own."

"Doggone," Boomer added, not understanding why his word choice drew a few laughs,

Whinestein asked, "Okay, what else is going on with our leader?"

"I haven't had a chance to tell you, but that camera that you hid in Al K. Bones office, I've been checking on the video. And I heard something."

"What-what-what…?"came out of the mouths of the pups.

"It was a one-way phone conversation with Bone mentioning a suspicious shipment of goods arriving at one his warehouses. I wanted my dad to know about it, so I left a note in his car. I'm pretty sure he acted on the tip, but I have no idea what happened and it's driving me bonkers." The pups took a minute to let this new information to set in.

"Anything else?" Brittany asked.

Roddy hesitated, then said, "Well, yes, but it's kind of between my dad, mom and me."

"You don't have to tell us." A few moments went by before Roddy spoke.

"Well, you guys know that there's a long line of police in my family?"

"And you're planning to follow in the Weiler tradition, right?"

"Well, I just found out that my mom wants me to be a lawyer."

In unison, the words came out,

"Oh, no… Not a lawyer!"

Chapter 17

The Devils Den

The unfinished room was an odd setting for the sophisticated medical equipment, barely visible in the dim light. An ominous line of large glass tanks draped in canvas lined the far wall. A single floodlight bathed the Salvador Collie painting resting unceremoniously against a brick wall.

A sinister figure in a white lab coat gestured dramatically and said, "Behold the result of your night out on the town." Screeching sounds poured out from the tanks, seemingly to acknowledge approval.

"Those dim-witted police dogs must be tearing their hair out, agonizing over the fate of their precious painting." The floodlight lit up his white lab coat in a ghostly, luminous glow and cast a grotesque shadow across the painting. His body was bent over with a pronounced hunch back that stood out under his lab coat. With the help of a thick, knobby cane, he moved closer to the painting. He pressed his angular face close to the canvas and studied it carefully.

"It's such an unpleasant setting for a masterpiece of a painting. Salvador Collie would be most displeased with me," he said unapologetically. He put his face close to the painting and bellowed,

"So sue me—hahahahaha" He stood back and continued to address the painting as if it was a living, breathing thing.

"Talk to me Salvador, you crazy, gifted artist. Share with me the secrets of your *Everlasting* painting." Disappointment crossed his face, as he half expected the lifeless painting to respond to his appeal.

"So you choose to remain silent. Well, we have ways to make you talk." His high-pitched laugh reverberated around the room. The glass tanks rattled in response, followed by a chorus of eerie screeching sounds. The odd figure walked to an ornate table and stared down on a large, ancient-looking, leather-bound book. He blew a coating of dust off the cover, revealing mystical raised symbols. He closed his eyes and ran his paw over the symbols, then seemed to drift into a trance. As his paws gently moved across the face of the book, they started to shake, and soon his entire body was trembling. Then in a blink, a calm settled over him. He stood motionless over the book for a few minutes and then his eyes popped open, breaking the trance.

"Well, that was a kick," he said mockingly to his unseen friends in the glass cages. "The book reveals that the eccentric artist discovered ancient secrets, which he cleverly translated to this painting."

His look intensified as he turned toward the painting, scanning every inch of canvas. He spoke as if the spirit of Salvador Collie haunted the painting.

"I know, you wacko genius, that somewhere hidden in your brush strokes is a clue that will lead me to a life-saving discovery. To complete my work, I must unravel your secrets." He sounded content, almost giddy. He walked over to a glass tank that stood alone.

"You did very well, my brave general. You and your soldiers deserve a little reward." Dr. Dingo lifted his cane and used it to press a button on the wall. A mechanical sound signaled the opening of a skylight in the ceiling, revealing the night sky. The sight of a full moon lighting up the room set off a wild celebration within the glass tanks.

Chapter 18

Lost Dog

Roddy and Boomer walked through the revolving doors of Vets Hospital. Roddy, posing as a reporter for his school's newspaper, had gotten Dr. Hindlick to grant an interview. It was Boomer's job to use his super-duper nose to sniff out the trail that Ollie took when he left the room. Roddy had considered using one of Whinestein's inventions for the job, but they agreed that the best tracking weapon in the pups' arsenal was Boomer's nose. Boomer led Roddy up the elevator and on to the floor where Ollie's room was located. Speeding down the hall, heading right at them, was the same patient who almost ran Boomer down on his last visit. Boomer grabbed a startled Roddy and shoved him against the wall as the wild wheelchair racer flew by, did a few wheelies, then sped on. Boomer shook his paw at the driver, and yelled, "Slow down! You're going to land someone in the hospital!"

"We are in the hospital, Boomer."

As they walked down the hall, Boomer continued to mumble under his breath, "Crazy driver. They should take his license away."

"Chill," Roddy said. When they reached the door of Ollie's room, yellow crime tape spanning the door frame blocked their way. Boomer eased his way through the crime tape.

"Okay Boomer, turn your sniffer on, and see if you can pick up Ollie's trail. I'm heading for Doc Hindlick's office. Hopefully the doc can shed some light on the case. Call me if you pick up Ollie's trail." Roddy left Boomer sniffing away in Buster's room.

As Boomer circled around the room, head bobbing up and down, his nose kicked into overdrive and soon a smug smile came over his face. He picked up Ollie's scent and followed it out of the room and down the hall to an emergency stairwell, all the while keeping a watchful eye out for the wacky wheelchair racer.

Roddy returned to the lobby; checked the directory and found Dr. Hindlick's name. He made a mental note of the room number and followed the signs. Roddy checked the big clock that hung on the wall and saw that he was on time for his appointment.

The door to Doctor Hindlick's office was partly open. Roddy knocked softly, and getting no response, pushed the door open. The office was empty. Roddy hesitated for a moment, checked up and down the hall, and then entered. It was a small office with a large, old-fashioned wooden desk dominating the space. Books and file folders cluttered the desk and spilled out on the floor. Books were also crammed into a bookcase that ran almost up to the ceiling. Roddy surveyed the walls that were covered with medical degrees and awards. He found a framed newspaper article that told the story of the doctor's discovery of the famous Hindlick Maneuver.

Of course, Roddy thought to himself. *If someone was eating too fast and started to choke, the 'Hindlick Maneuver' could save their life.* Roddy recalled the time when Boomer was gulping down biscuits so fast that he started to gasp for air. Fortunately, Whinestein darted across the room and used the Hindlick Maneuver to dislodge a biscuit stuck in his throat. Roddy shuddered to think what could have happened if Whinestein hadn't moved so quickly. "Thank you Dr. Hindlick, for helping to save my friend."

A framed degree caught Roddy's attention. Dr. Hindlick had earned a master's degree in the science of entomology. *Dr. Hindlick, not only have you distinguished yourself in the medical field, but you just became a suspect in the theft of the Salvador Collie painting.*

Even though he had his share of fleabites, Roddy had always been interested in the fascinating world of insects. Roddy thought that this revelation of Dr. Hindlick's specialty might have brought him a step closer to solving the mystery.

Roddy's Doggie Talkie vibrated. "What is it, Boomer?"

Boomer was nervously panting and whispered, "Take the stairwell down the hall from Ollie's room. When you get to the top, look for a sign that says, 'Stairway closed for repairs'. Disregard the sign and…Roddy, I can't…" Roddy heard a clatter of Boomer's Doggie Talkie falling to the floor—and the line fell silent.

Roddy raced out of the room. The meeting with Dr. Hindlick would have to wait. He spotted the exit sign leading to the stairwell, threw open the door, and tore up the stairs. When Roddy reached the seventh floor, the steps came to an end. 'Stairway closed for repairs' was stenciled across a board blocking the stairwell. He opened the door to the seventh floor and looked around. The floor was dedicated to patient rooms. He hurried up and down the hallway but saw nothing out of the ordinary.

"Excuse me," he asked a passing nurse, "is there a way to get up to the top floor?"

"This is the top floor," she replied. Roddy ran back into the stairwell and took out his Doggie Talkie.

"Brittany, where are you?"

"I'm at the lab, on the computer. What's up?"

"We've got trouble here. Pull up the architectural drawings of Vets Hospital. Hurry!" Roddy paced impatiently on the landing of the stairway.

"Okay, I've got it."

"Just tell me how many floors show up on the drawings?"

"Seven…seven floors. One second. There seems to be a structure above the seventh floor. Hold on."

"Just hurry."

"Got it. It's in the architect's notes. Seems like they ran out of funds and the top floor was never completed. What's going on?"

"Boomer's missing…no time to talk."

"What?"

Roddy felt a chill, not just from the dampness in the stairwell, but from a strange eeriness that crept over him.

There's got to be a way to get up there somehow, Roddy thought to himself as he tapped the wall…nothing. He then rubbed his paw along the cinder block wall of the stairway.

"Got it," he said, pulling out a loose block. Inside the opening was a lever. He stepped back to review his options when he felt a stab of pain on the back of his neck. He staggered against the cinder block wall, his head spinning, and finally… blackness.

Chapter 19

Roddy's Nightmare

Roddy was powerless to move any part of his body. His eyelids were too heavy to open, but his mind was exploding with vivid images. He was playing fetch with his father, running wildly through a grassy field chasing birds, barking as they took flight. The scene quickly shifted to the vet's office. Roddy's head rested on his mom's lap as she gently stroked his tummy, easing his fear of the impending puppy shots. Then he was half dozing on a spongy carpet of grass, stretched out on his back, soaking in the warm rays of the sun.

Suddenly, the pleasurable images burst apart like a broken jigsaw puzzle. A fog rolled in, and with it came a sense of doom. Roddy struggled to hang on to the more tender scenes, but lost the battle as he found himself in the middle of his worst nightmare.

"Nooo…." He cried out. He saw himself chained to a solitary tree sitting on a hilltop. The tree was bare of leaves and the gnarled branches seemed to grab at him like the tentacles of a giant octopus. The sky was dark and ominous. But the worst was yet to come. He stared in horror as a hoard of insects with fiery eyes and flailing antenna crawled menacingly toward him. He strained against the heavy chains, but they were unyielding.

Then the sky grew darker as swarms of flying insects dove at him in perfect formation. They peeled off just a few feet from the helpless pup and then circled back again and again. Wave after wave swarmed around his head, hundreds of stingers poised to attack his body. The intensity of flapping wings was deafening.

"Nooo…" Roddy's scream was lost in the din of the screeching and buzzing that surrounded him. The chains dug into his body as he fought desperately to free himself as the invading insect hordes closed in.

"Ugh!" His cries were never heard outside of his own head. Then, suddenly, the nightmare dissolved from his thoughts. Gone were the creatures with their blazing eyes. Silence replaced the screeching sounds of the swarming insects. The fog drifted away.

Roddy stirred, relieved that he was once again in control of his senses. He pawed at his neck where the stab of pain had preceded his horrifying hallucinations. He cautiously opened his eyes and found himself in a cage. He surveyed his surroundings, which in the dim light appeared to be a medical laboratory. And there it was. The imposing Salvador Collie painting resting against a bare brick wall, bathed in the unflattering illumination of a floodlight. For a long moment, he stared at the painting, hypnotized by its bold colors and shapes.

Salvador Collie would flip out if he saw his painting propped up against a brick wall. He twisted his body to take in a broader view of the laboratory. Looking up, he observed a skylight. The moon was dimmed by grime-covered windowpanes.

Roddy reached into his pocket for his Doggie Talkie but it was gone. There was no way for Roddy to communicate with the outside world. He squinted through the dimness and saw other cages similar to his own. His heart nearly stopped when he spotted Boomer lying in a cage, thrashing around. Roddy imagined that he, too, was being abused by a frightful nightmare. He softly called his name, "Boomer, Boomer," but got no response. He reached through the bars of his cage to touch Boomer, but could not stretch far enough. Boomer's thrashing at least gave Roddy some comfort that his friend was still alive.

Roddy heard incoherent mumbling and turned to see, who he presumed was Ollie McNally. The museum guard was propped up against the bars of his cage—his leg twitching uncontrollably. Ollie was still dressed in his white hospital gown. A deep red stain fanned out on the thick bandage wrapped around his head.

The Lunatick

Looking past Ollie, Roddy was surprised to see yet another cage. The light that reflected from the Collie painting didn't quite reach to the far cage, but Roddy's keen eyes made out a figure slumped awkwardly against the bars. He had no idea of the identity of the victim, but, knew he was one more victim of a mad dog. Roddy was adjusting to the faint light of his surroundings. He searched the room, taking inventory of anything that might be helpful in planning an escape.

His ears perked up as he heard the low din of screeching coming from behind glass tanks stacked against the far wall. Roddy's sense of doom intensified when he realized that he could be facing multiple numbers of deadly creatures. The shock of their reality once again touched off frightful images in his head. He cried out, as he imagined his eyes springing out from his head and zooming across the room to the glass cages; coming face to face with the devil itself. With his mind playing tricks, blazing eyes locked on to Roddy holding him captive. His heart pounded in fear.

Get me out of this nightmare, he pleaded, shaking his head to clear the horrifying image. He blinked hard, and suddenly the 'devil' disappeared.

Roddy had no idea how much time had passed since he found himself captive in the cage. He fought to focus on the events that had brought him to this terrifying moment. Roddy Weiler was a very brave pup, but still he was a pup, and at no time in his short life had he faced such peril.

Roddy racked his brain for answers. Minutes passed.

"The painting! It's got to be in the painting. But where to start?" Roddy's eyes focused on the canvas as he studied the swirling colors and strange symbols. He searched every inch of the canvas probing for clues. Roddy thought about Brittany and Boomer's strange encounter with Ollie in his hospital room. "I've got to get through to Ollie." He glanced over at Ollie and spoke to him as if we were an attentive listener. "Hey, Ollie! Mr. McNally! What is it with this painting? Help us out? Please?"

Getting no response, he barked out, "Ollie! Open your damn eyes!"

But Ollie/Salvador remained silent.

Chapter 20

Security

The automatic doors leading into Vets Hospital swung open. Rod surveyed the lobby. It was buzzing with visitors carrying flowers and neatly wrapped gifts to cheer patients on the upper floors.

"Busy place. Must be having a sale," Rod quipped.

"I hear that they offer a cut rate price on neutering," Germaine said seriously, then laughed at the sight of the tough detective squirming.

"Captain Shepherd?" Germaine felt a big paw on her shoulder and turned. "I'm Monty Mastiff, head of security." Mastiff was as wide as he was tall, ripped with muscle that bulged out from his tight-fitting uniform. Forget the bulk, though—the perpetual scowl on his face was enough to intimidate. His steely eyes said, *Don't mess with my hospital.*

Mastiff led Germaine and Rod through a series of hallways

The Lunatick

stretching out from the hospital lobby. The administrative wing was at the heart of the hospital and what made this venerable institution tick. Mastiff had little to say until they reached a door with *Conference Room B* stenciled on a frosted glass panel. It was bare of the amenities found in most medical offices. The rising cost of health care caused many cutbacks at the hospital, and this was reflected in the austere look of the room: pale green cinder block walls, worn linoleum floor, and sparse metal furniture. Adding a little luster to the room was a young nurse who was seated at the end of a conference table. She rose as the visitors entered.

"Lolly Pup," Mastiff said, "Captain Shepherd, Detective Weiler." Rod sized up the nervous young lady. She had a pretty face, but the lines around her puffy eyes showed fatigue. Her nurse's cap was cocked at an odd angle and her uniform was disheveled. A splatter of dried fluid was noticeable on her sleeve. It looked like she had just come off of a long shift and this was the last place that she wanted to be.

"Lolly was the duty nurse responsible for the museum guard today," Mastiff said. Germaine acknowledged Lolly with a nod then turned to Mastiff.

"Will Ollie's doctor be joining us?" Monty Mastiff hesitated then murmured, "No, I'm sorry."

"We were assured that Dr. Hindlick would be here," Rod sounded annoyed.

Mastiff shot a quick look at Lolly. She took the cue and

responded hesitantly, "We don't know where he is." Mastiff studied the puzzled looks on the faces of the visitors.

"It seems," he measured his words carefully, "that Dr. Hindlick has… disappeared."

"He didn't sign out and his beeper was turned off," Lolly's voice trailed off. "It's not like him."

"Dr. Hindlick is one of our oldest-tenured doctors," Mastiff said. "Very well respected and brilliant."

"So now we have a missing museum guard and a missing doctor," Germaine said. One look at Monty Mastiff's face showed that he took this breakdown very seriously. A witness to a serious crime had been abducted right out of his hospital bed and one of his docs was missing. No way could he play nursemaid to every doctor in the hospital, but bad things were happening on his watch and he felt responsible.

Rod sat down next to Lolly and said in a reassuring voice, "Tell us what you know about Ollie McNally's disappearance."

"It's been a very busy day and we're short on nurses. The patient load was heavy and the patient in 725 needed constant attention."

"The patient in 725 is Ollie McNally?" Rod asked.

Lolly nodded and continued, "He was in a great deal of discomfort and hallucinating most of the day."

"Did Ollie say anything that might give us a clue to his disappearance?" Germaine asked.

"He said a lot, but most of the time he was just ranting in Spanish. I couldn't understand him at all."

"Spanish?" Rod asked skeptically. Lolly shrugged her shoulders.

"Think hard, were there any unusual events that occurred during your shift that could explain his disappearance?" Germaine inquired.

"I can't think of anything, but I feel some responsibility for what happened. He was my patient," Lolly hardly finished the sentence when the tears started. The tough head of security walked over, placed his paw on her shoulder, handed her a tissue, then said a few soothing words.

Rod asked, "Besides his unsettling mental state, how was his physical condition?"

Lolly dabbed at the tears running down her cheek and composed herself. "He has typical symptoms of severe head trauma. We had trouble stopping the bleeding from the head wound and had to change the dressing several times. He lost considerable blood and needed a transfusion."

"Did he have any visitors?" Germaine asked.

"I was just taking a break when a couple of pups showed up. May have been relatives, I'm not sure. When I saw Dr. Hindlick later in the day, he asked about the pups, but they left before Ollie disappeared."

Germaine asked, "When did you last see Dr. Hindlick?"

Lolly looked at her watch, "About three hours ago. It's been a very hectic day and I'm exhausted. My shift was over hours ago. Can I go now?"

Germaine looked at Rod, who nodded.

"Sure, but we may want to talk to you again," Germaine said. Without saying a word, Lolly hurried out of the room. Germaine turned to Mastiff. "We need to talk to Dr. Hindlick. Do you have any idea what could have happened to him?"

"Our security personnel searched every inch of the hospital. We sent someone to his home, but no luck. We checked the parking lot and his Land Rover is still in its reserved spot." Mastiff thought for a moment. "It just seems too much of a coincidence that Mr. McNally and Dr. Hindlick would both turn up missing within hours of each other."

"Are you suggesting that the doctor may have had something to do with Ollie's disappearance?" Germaine asked.

"I don't want to point a paw at anyone, but Hindlick's sort of strange guy. He's a good doctor, but he has some unusual interests."

"Like what?" Rod asked.

"Like, he gets all weird on the subject of bugs."

Rod jumped to his feet and was halfway out the door, "Take us to Dr. Hindlick's office."

Chapter 21

Like Caged Animals

Roddy was thinking through the events of the day when he noticed an ancient looking leather book; it's cover adorned with bizarre symbols on a small table near the painting. Thinking to himself, *That book, could it provide clues to this nightmare?*

A series of low moans interrupted Roddy's thoughts. He glanced toward Boomer, but he was not moving. Ollie seemed to have regained consciousness, but had not completely shaken the venom that was playing havoc with his head. Roddy realized the moaning was coming from the stranger's cage. Slowly the stranger sat up and looked around, trying to focus on his surroundings, struggling to get his bearings. His glazed eyes settled on Roddy.

Roddy asked, "Who are you, sir?"

The stranger hesitated, trying to focus on Roddy, "My name is…Hindlick."

"What? Dr. Hindlick?" The doctor nodded.

"Cross him off as a suspect," Roddy mumbled. Roddy waited for the doctor to gather his thoughts.

"Who are you? How did I get here? What happened?" The doctor slurred the questions.

It took Roddy a few minutes to fill in the blanks for Dr. Hindlick.

The doctor slumped back against the corner of the cage and tried to absorb the astonishing events just related to him.

"A genetically altered mutant insect?" he asked.

Roddy doubted that there was very little that Dr. Hindlick didn't know about insects, but obviously the idea of an altered insect was a shock to him.

"You saw this ..." Hindlick hesitated, ..."thing? Can you described what it looked like?"

Roddy thought for a moment. He scratched his head, trying to sort out the horror that flashed through his mind before the venom had dispersed. He closed his eyes as a vision of the creature appeared.

Roddy spoke hesitantly, "Well actually, the venom was playing games with my head. I may have imagined it, but I'm not sure."

"I don't understand," Dr. Hindlick was clearly confused.

"I don't get it, either, Doc, but it sure took over my brain." Roddy closed his eyes and shared his illusion. "It had eight legs, crab-like claws—a tick-like creature, but much larger." Roddy hesitated as a chill ran up his spine. "Those eyes—those bulging, blazing eyes—will spook me like forever"

"My young friend, the creature's venom is obviously very powerful and is capable of producing hallucinations. It seems that it effects its victims in different ways. Fortunately, the hallucinations that I encountered did not include such horrific images."

As Dr. Hindlick finished his sentence, a flash of lightning burst through the skylight, followed by a loud crash of thunder. As if lighting and thunder didn't scare the dogs enough, it also set off blood-curdling screeching from the direction of the tanks as the creatures threw themselves against the glass. An astonished Dr. Hindlick fell back in his cage and stammered, "There must be a dozens of those creatures—maybe hundreds."

Soon the screeching stopped and, once again, silence filled the room, except for some distant sounds of thunder. It took the terrified captives quite a while before they could compose themselves. Finally Dr Hindlick spoke up.

"The arachnid conference, of course. I remember now. Several years ago, many of the great minds in the field of entomology gathered at a conference. The featured subject was a discussion on how the warming of the planet was affecting insects, particularly those in the arachnid family. There was one scientist who presented a study that showed how he could genetically combine the DNA of different species to create a new specimen never before seen in the insect world."

"What do you know about this scientist?" Roddy asked.

"He was an odd fellow. He made a preposterous claim that he could take the DNA of several varieties of deadly spiders and scorpions and combine them with the DNA of a garden-variety tick. I recall one of the test species was a funnel-web spider, which is distinctive by the way it stands up on its hind legs, exposing its fangs. The spider possesses a neurotoxic venom that could kill its victims."

"So, is it possible that by implanting a sack of spider or scorpion venom into the body of a tick could turn it into some kind of a Frankenbug?"

"As a professor of entomology, it's hard for me to believe such a thing is possible. But the doctor who made the presentation was quite persuasive that he had the scientific know-how to pull it off. Indeed, we could be looking at a dangerous, super-toxic tick," Hindlick said, glancing apprehensively at the row of tanks across the room. "The concept was ridiculed by everyone in attendance, and I recall that the scientist stomped off stage after an angry outburst."

"Do you remember the name of this ... tick doc?"

"Tick doc...funny," Boomer chuckled, forgetting for the moment how dire their situation was.

Hindlick took a few moments to run through his memory bank, "Sorry, I can't remember his name."

A voice from the other side of the room boomed out, "Could the name of that tick doc be Dingo. Dr. Max Dingo?"

Chapter 22

Live or Die

A figure in a white lab coat, carrying a thick cane emerged from the shadows. Everything about Dr. Dingo looked sinister. His dark eyes were narrow and sunken into his craggy face, and drool seeped from his mouth. He was a large breed, but walked with a stoop that drew attention to the hump on his back.

"So, you've become acquainted with the chorus of my arachnid experiment. Scary… huh? Well, you haven't seen the full rage of my little army. Quite by accident I discovered that when my subjects were exposed to moonlight, a strange metamorphosis took place. The DNA exchanges that I made were dramatically enhanced when the fullness of the moon swept over their bodies." Dr. Dingo made a sweeping gesture toward the glass tanks. "It caused my little ones to have quite a growth spurt and you, my guests, may soon get to meet them up close and personal."

"You and your experiments are brilliant," Dr. Hindlick said. "But please, this is evil. Why can't you use your brilliant mind to do good for all of dogkind."

"So touching," Dr. Dingo said, pretending to wipe a tear from his eye. "You and your high and mighty friends ridiculed and humiliated me in front of the entire scientific community." He raised his cane menacingly in the air. "You laughed me off the stage in the middle of my presentation and that ticked me off." "Get it! TICK-ed me off…hahahahaha." His manic laugh reverberated around the room and raised the level of screeching behind the glass.

Dr. Hindlick raised his voice, "What do you want with us?"

Dr. Dingo playfully cupped his paw over his ear, "I can't hear you."

"He's playing us, doc." Roddy said.

"I assure you, this is not a party game, my young friend."

When Roddy saw the hatred in Dr. Dingo's bloodshot eyes, he realized that the odds of escaping from this place of horrors were even worse than he'd thought. But he refused to give up hope.

The sudden activity in the room brought Boomer out of his disoriented state. He awoke with a loud yawn—seemingly, his nightmare behind him. His mind-set changed quickly as he stared through the bars of his cage and into Dr. Dingo's angry eyes.

"Yikes," he cried out, backing into the farthest corner of

his cage.

"Did you have a pleasant nap, my young friend?" Dr. Dingo asked in a most gentle voice.

Boomer, still shaky from the venom injected into his body, was very confused. "Yes…no …I think so?"

"You may wish that you never awakened."

Boomer's eyes darted around the room, quickly assessing his nightmarish predicament. He shot a glance at Roddy, searching for answers. Roddy's face was reassuring and calm.

"Well, let's see," Dr Dingo said. "All of the players in this little game have risen from their slumber, except our friend the museum guard."

Putting his fears aside, Roddy said coyly, "Dr Dingo, can you tell us why you went to so much trouble to steal the painting and what do you want of us?"

"Patience, my young friend—patience."

Roddy tried playing to the demented doctor's huge ego. "Your experiment on arachnids is awesome. But consider what your creepy ticks would do if they escaped from this room. It would be a disaster for Collywood."

A devilish look appeared on Dingo's face and he said matter-of-factly,

"Exactly."

"You are not well, Dr. Dingo," Dr. Hindlick said. "You don't have to do this, I can help you."

The comment enraged Dingo. He raised his gnarled cane and raked it against the bars of Hindlick's cage, then jabbed the cane at Hindlick through the bars. Hindlick cowered in the back of the cage, trying to ward off Dingo's thrusts.

Roddy shouted over the din of the heavy cane meeting the metal of the cage. "How can we help you?"

Dingo turned to face Roddy, his cane held threateningly. Roddy was unflinching and calmly repeated, "How can we help you?" Roddy's soothing voice seemed to settle Dr. Dingo for the moment.

He said, less belligerently, "Yes, that's a good question. There are secrets hidden in the brushstrokes of Salvador Collie's painting. Secrets so mind-boggling that they could make the difference between life or death for me…for you." That sent chills up and down the spines of the captives.

"Because of his obsession with Collie's painting, Ollie McNally will be the key to solve this puzzle. Unfortunately, you and your chubby little friend have become collateral damage. You were at the wrong place at the wrong time. Although, you could be useful in helping to reveal the painting's secrets."

"Why am I here?" Dr Hindlick asked, already knowing what the answer will be.

"You, Dr. Hindlick, were one of the scientists who belittled my work and laughed me off the stage. For that," he said gleefully, "you will be a treat for my hungry horde behind the glass." Dr. Hindlick contemplating his fate, slumped back in his cage.

"Let me get this straight," Roddy said."You want us… rather you need us to decipher the secrets hidden in Salvador Collie's painting."

"You impress me, my young pup. Yes, I need your help and yes, there is a message hidden in the painting."

"What makes you so sure?" Roddy asked.

Dr. Dingo placed his hand on the mysterious book, and said, "It's in the book, my friend, it's in the book." Dr. Dingo's face suddenly went blank as he seemed to fall into a deep trance. Minutes passed with all eyes on the motionless doctor.

Then, suddenly, he snapped out of his trance and said, "I have an important assignment for you. If you succeed, I can promise you a nice reward." Dingo stared grimly at the group.

"Here's the deal—I'm going to excuse myself and while I'm gone, I want your little group to work with the museum guard to solve the puzzle and you better hope that he soon regains his senses." As Dr. Dingo slowly hobbled away, Boomer bravely called after to him.

"What's the reward?"

Dr. Dingo stopped. He turned around and in a cold, steely voice said,

"Your life—isn't that the best reward?"

Boomer's head nervously bobbed up and down.

"However, if you fail to come up with an answer to this spellbinding riddle …" Dr. Dingo's eyes narrowed. He pointed his cane menacingly in the direction of the glass tanks. "Let's say that my blood-thirsty friends will have a special dinner tonight."

Boomer started to shake so vigorously that his cage began to rattle. Roddy shot a look at him and mouthed the words, *No fear. Show no fear.* Boomer got the message, but his round body continued to shake out of control.

Roddy turned back to Dr. Dingo, but he was gone.

Chapter 23

Putting the Squeeze on Al K. Bone

Rod and PD Captain Shepherd, accompanied by two uniformed police dogs, pounded the ornate knocker on the door of Al K. Bone's home.

Germaine barked out, "Open the door! Collywood PD!"

Rod was getting ready to throw his weight against the door, when it swung open. Al K. Bone stood at the door.

"What makes you think that you can just barge into my home like this?"

Rod stuck the judge's court order in Bone's face and pushed his way in. Another one of Bone's goons stepped between the two and with paws clenched Rod and the guard stared each other down. "Go ahead animal, make a move. Give us an excuse to toss you in the pen."

The Lunatick

Bone finally waved off the guard.

"Okay, have your fun," Bone said reluctantly as he led the police through a long hallway to his library. "I'll return in a moment," Bone said as he left the room. Rod and Germaine gawked at the designer leather chairs and plush throw rugs that covered dark paneled wood floors. The shelves along the walls were lined with rows of books, Rod was sure that Bone had never read any of them.

"Crime does pay, I guess." Rod said sarcastically, He scanned the rows of books, and pulled out one at random.

"Return that book to the shelf," Bone barked out as he entered the room accompanied by a fancy looking breed. "That book is a first edition of an F. Scott Spitzgerald *The Great Dane.*"

"Bought or stolen?" Rod said seriously. The long-time foes used their eyes to throw daggers at each other. Bone introduced his attorney, Flea Bailey to Captain Shepherd.

"Flea Bailey is very well known down at Collywood PD." Germaine said .

"Hotshot attorney to the stars," Rod said with disdain. "And, to every dirty dog in town—that can afford him."

Flea Bailey was a highly talented lawyer who represented high-profile celebrities. In fact, Flea Bailey was a celebrity in his own right; a well-known media hound who craved the spotlight. His fame took off when he defended dogfather Lucky Lassieano in a trial that was one of Collywood's most high-profile cases. Once bitter rivals, Lassieano and Al K. Bone had agreed to settle their differences and divide up their criminal enterprises in Collywood. The two dogfathers, for the moment, were at peace following a bloody gang war.

With his slicked-back hair, neatly trimmed facial hair, and his very expensive pin-stripped suit, Flea Bailey cut an imposing figure.

"Hello Rod and nice to see you again Captain Shepherd," Bailey said politely. "Mr Bone has already provided his testimony on the warehouse incident, and I've advised him not to discuss the alleged incident further."

"Yes, we'll see you in court on that action, but we're here to discuss a different case." Germaine said.

"Wait, are you still trying to pin the Petropolitan Museum heist on me?" Bone asked sarcastically. Captain Shepherd reached into her bag and pulled out a photograph.

"Recognize this?"

"Ahh yes, the missing Salvador Collie painting—sorry, but you're barking up the wrong tree if you think it's in my possession."

"We'll see about that," Rod said. "Our court order allows us to search your home." Bailey took the court order from Rod and read the document. Bailey nodded approval of the legitimacy of the court order.

"I doubt if you'll find any bodies lying around, but go ahead and search your tails off."

The police dogs spread out to search the house. It took most of the day, with the police snapping photographs of Bone's vast art collection. Jack Russell, the Petropolitan Museum's curator joined the group to inventory Al K. Bone's collection. Rod felt that the odds were low that Collie's *Everlasting* painting would turn up at Bone's home, but he didn't rule out that it could be stashed in a hidden vault somewhere in the mansion.

Although they left the mansion empty handed, Rod delighted in making life as miserable as possible for Bone.

Chapter 24

Hypnotic Spell

Roddy fought to get his emotions under control. If there was any chance to get out of this peril, he needed a clear head. He quickly evaluated his resources: the strengths of his fellow captives. Good old Boomer had a talented nose for following a trail, but a good sniffer wasn't going to rescue them from this nightmare. Dr. Hindlick knew a lot about insects, but could he be trusted to hold up under this pressure cooker? The key player in Dr. Dingo's deadly game was Ollie and his mystifying connection to Collie's painting. His quick recovery was crucial to their survival. He had to wake up Ollie.

"Ollie, snap out of it!" Roddy shouted. He rattled his cage and banged the bars, trying desperately to shake Ollie out of his stupor. Hindlick and Boomer followed Roddy's lead and hammered away at the bars of their cages. The racket agitated the ticks and they joined the noisy chorus with earsplitting screeching. Ollie finally stirred. He shot up, hitting his injured head against the top of the cage. He cried out and grabbed his head as a pattern of new blood showed through bandages. Roddy held up his paw to stop the banging on the bars. Soon the screeching of the restless ticks settled into a low buzz. Ollie searched the faces of the other captives looking for answers. As he tried desperately to get his bearings, a few unrecognizable words sputtered from his mouth.

Roddy said gently, "Go easy, Ollie. Take a few minutes to clear your head."

Ollie looked at his fellow captives, then his eyes focused on Boomer. There was a hint of recognition. Boomer smiled pleasantly and waited to see what language would flow from his mouth.

"Where am I?" Ollie asked, speaking in good old English.

"I'm Dr. Hindlick—I've been taking care of you since your accident at the museum."

"Except it wasn't an accident." Roddy said." You were the victim of a pretty weird crime."

Ollie shook his head trying to clear the cobwebs. A few senseless images flooded his head. Then just as suddenly, the image of Spike, in his deranged state crossed his mind and wouldn't leave.

"Spike!" Ollie howled in despair. "What happened to Spike?"

"Ollie, calm down." Dr. Hindlick said. "Spike is fine and probably just as bewildered as you are."

"I'll fill you in with the details later, but right now…" Roddy gestured toward the painting, "We need you to concentrate on the Salvador Collie painting."

Like recognizing an old friend, Ollie's awareness of the painting appeared to give him some comfort. He stared at the colorful canvas, and then closed his eyes. Roddy hoped that seeing his favorite painting would take Ollie back to his familiar museum setting. Ollie remained motionless. Roddy rattled the bars of his cage once more and shouted, "Ollie, come back! We need you here on earth." Ollie's eyes opened slowly, pleading for answers. Roddy described the horrifying events of the past few days. Ollie's look of confusion suddenly turned to fear.

"Hey, amigo," Boomer said showing off the extent of his Spanish. "In the hospital room, you were spurting out a bunch of stuff in Spanish. What was that all about?"

Ollie looked baffled. "Spanish? I don't speak Spanish."

Dr. Hindlick explained how some head injury patients have been known to quite unexpectedly converse in a language that was previously unfamiliar to them.

"Ollie, what is it about the Salvador Collie painting that has you so obsessed?" Hindlick asked. "You have spent many hours at the museum completely absorbed in his masterpiece."

Ollie stared hard at the canvas, which shimmered under the high-density light.

Dr. Hindlick continued, "Your fascination with the painting. Your sudden fluency in a new language caused from your serious head injury. All of this tricked you into thinking that you were…" he hesitated, "…the brilliant Spanish painter, Salvador Collie."

"Heavy," Boomer said.

"Heavy indeed," Roddy repeated. "I think you're right on, Doc, and if we're going to untangle this challenge we need Ollie with a clear head."

"We're doomed!" Boomer said hopelessly.

"Maybe not," Dr. Hindlick said. "I might be able to break through to Ollie's sub-conscious mind by putting him into a hypnotic trance. Ollie, have you ever been hypnotized?"

Ollie placed his paws to his bandaged head. "I don't think so. Right now my head is really messed up."

"Ollie, there are no harmful effects with hypnosis, and if you allow me to do this, there's a chance that it could save lives,"

"Ours." Boomer added.

Dr. Hindlick continued. "Basically, hypnosis uses intense concentration to achieve a heightened state of awareness. It is sometimes called a trance. Everything around the subject is temporarily blocked out."

Ollie took a few moments to take it all in, then nodded his approval.

"Go for it, Doc," Roddy said. Dr. Hindlick removed the shiny dog tag that hung on his collar and dangled it in Ollie's direction. His voice was soft and calming. The dog tag shimmered from the light that flooded the painting. Ollie's eyes focused on the tag and he quickly fell into a hypnotic state.

"Can you hear me?"

"Yes, I hear you, doctor," Ollie mumbled in a sleepy voice.

"Yes, I hear you, doctor." Boomer said.

"Boomer, wake up," Roddy barked. "You're not the one being hypnotized."

Boomer opened his eyes, oblivious to his momentary hypnotic trance. Dr. Hindlick turned his attention back to Ollie.

"What is your name?"

There was a long pause, " Me llamo…Salvador Collie."

"Success!" Roddy bellowed.

"So, you're the famous Salvador Collie?" Dr. Hindlick asked.

"Si señor," Ollie said with deep pride in his voice.

"Mi amigo, is that canvas on the wall one of your paintings?" Ollie nodded. "I must say, it's a brilliant work of art. May I call you Salvador?" Ollie nodded again. "Salvador, your work is a gift for all art lovers, but there is a deeper meaning to your work, isn't that right?"

"Si." Ollie stared intently at the painting for several minutes and then said in a thoughtful voice. "Simbolos…simbolos." Another few minutes ticked off before Ollie spoke again. "Ballena…Colibrí…Pulpo…Rana…Mariposa."

"What's that all about?" An inquisitive Boomer asked.

"It's Spanish, Boomer." Dr. Hindlick said. "I believe he said the word 'symbols' several times, but I didn't understand the other words." Dr. Hindlick waited a few moments before asking Ollie. "Can you tell us what those symbols mean?" Ollie's voice fell silent.

After a few minutes, it was clear that Ollie was not ready to disclose any more information. Dr. Hindlick snapped Ollie out of his hypnotic state, then surprisingly Ollie spoke clearly to the caged group.

'Whale, hummingbird, octopus, frog, butterfly.'

Roddy shifted his gaze to the painting. "Great, our first clue, but what does it all mean?"

Dr. Hindlick said, scratching his hairy chin, "If my memory serves me correctly, ancient cultures believed that animals were powerful dream symbols; representing our emotions, fears, and hopes. Civilizations through the years used animal symbols to tell stories and fables."

Boomer exclaimed, "It's in the book. That's what Dr. Dingo said." All eyes shifted to the mysterious book on the table.

The captives contemplated the unreachable distance from table to cage. Despair hung over the room.

So near, yet so far away, Roddy thought. Roddy's face brightened suddenly. His paw brushed against the pen-like device in his pocket. He pulled it out and murmured, "Whinestein, you're a genius." He clicked the button on Whinestein's latest invention and the long flexible end of the Wandering Wand flew through the bars and slashed wildly around the room.

Roddy's keen mind soon took full control of the wand. Hindlick, Boomer, and Ollie looked on in amazement as they followed the dancing wand. With its piercing light guiding the way, Roddy spun the wand around and hooked it to the leg of the table holding the leather-bound book. Slowly he coaxed the wand back to his cage, dragging the table with it. When it got within reach, Roddy carefully lifted the book off the table and brought it into the cage.

"Dr. Hindlick," Roddy said. "See if you can get anything more out of Ollie while I curl up with a good book." Roddy flipped through the pages of the centuries old, leather-bound book that told the story of Native legends and symbols.

Roddy realized that time was running out for his caged friends. Even with the brilliant mind of Dr. Hindlick and his knowledge of entomology, the task before them was daunting. *What was Dr. Dingo expecting to find in the Salvador Collie painting? What was the link between the dusty old book and the painting that could possibly save their lives?*

One thing was certain: they needed answers to an impossible puzzle. If they failed, it would be dinnertime for the little monsters that Dingo created.

Chapter 25

Symbols

Roddy's hopes were dashed. The book was written in a strange language that he could not understand. Then suddenly, MAGIC; right before his eyes, the illegible words faded away only to reappear as readable text. The first few pages turned out to be a primer on ancient Native symbols.

• • •

In the earliest of cultures, people were at the mercy of nature. To try to influence nature, they created various rituals and ceremonies. To preserve the knowledge of how these rituals were conducted, a teacher passed it on to his apprentices. Because of concerns that something could happen to the teacher before he could train others, they used pictures to share the ceremonies. The earliest writing was in the form of drawings of animals and people. The pictures of animals were attempts to appease the spirits of the animals that the group intended to hunt and kill.

Gradually, over time, early cultures shaped messages in the form of symbols. In ancient Egypt, they were called hieroglyphics. The cliff paintings of Native Americans were called petroglyphs because they were written on stone. They were created to communicate ritual information, assist travelers along trade routes, and for a number of other things. Although few Native American tribal groups spoke each other's languages, the petroglyphs were surprisingly standard throughout the various tribes.

As writing became more a part of the culture of most civilizations, issues of privacy developed. If the written word was intended only for the eyes of a few, the way to conceal a message was to create codes: symbols or groups of letters to represent words or phrases. Both the sender and recipient needed a codebook for more complex messages. The sender forwarded a coded message and the recipient translated the letters or symbols by studying his own codebook.

Historically, works of art—particularly surrealistic art—contained indirect messages, often in the form of symbols. Concerns and feelings were expressed through symbols that were often concealed in the paintings. Trying to determine the artist's true message was like solving a mystery. Part of the enjoyment in studying the works of some of the world's great artists is to explore for hidden meaning.

Symbols have played an important role in the art of many cultures. Native Americans, in particular, used animal symbols to tell colorful stories and to convey messages. AGAIN, AGREE

• • •

As Roddy studied the pages of the book, he glanced from the painting to the book. All eyes were locked on Roddy. They waited patiently to see if he would be able to pick up any clues that could give them some hope of survival. Roddy was captivated by the wisdom and prose that streamed from the pages of this mystical book. When he turned to the next chapter, the words that he was searching for literally jumped off the page.

'Whale, hummingbird, octopus, frog, butterfly.'

Roddy read on for a few more pages, then said to his fellow captives, "Do you remember the drawings in puzzle books when you were really young pups? We had to find hidden objects somewhere in the picture."

They all nodded.

"Well, we have our own little puzzle, and because Salvador Collie was able to get into Ollie's head, we have some pretty good clues." Roddy looked to Ollie and asked, "Ollie, can you run through that list of symbols again?"

The Lunatick

Ollie registered only confusion.

"I remember," Boomer said excitedly. "Whale... Hummingbird... Frog... " He hesitated.

Dr. Hindlick completed the list, "Octopus and Butterfly."

"That's right," Roddy said, "now, let's play the picture game and try to locate these symbols in the painting."

Roddy picked up the open book and extended it through the bars to give the others a better look. "They won't appear as exact replicas, rather they will show up as symbols like what you see on these pages." All eyes focused on the open book and then they turned to study the painting.

Boomer repeated the names slowly, "Whale... Hummingbird... Frog..."

He turned again to Dr. Hindlick for help and the doctor obliged, "Octopus and Butterfly."

Ollie, who seemed to be more coherent, shouted out, "The whale, there, in the lower corner!" There was great excitement as the appearance of the symbols suddenly seemed so obvious.

"The eyes can play tricks with the mind," Dr. Hindlick explained. "The symbols, which seemingly were hidden from view, now appear to jump off the canvas."

"There—upper right corner, the octopus!" Boomer shouted.

"Where?"

"Look closely. It's an upside-down octopus."

"I see it. I see it." A lull followed as all eyes searched the canvas.

"Look, a frog," Dr. Hindlick said in his controlled manner.

"Yes, the frog, almost hopped off the canvas," Roddy said with a smile. "Now, where is the butterfly?" In no time, all the symbols were located and Roddy was busy flipping through the pages of the book. As each symbol was found, Roddy explained its meaning as revealed in the book.

"Whale—the power of water, regeneration, life, and death."

"Hummingbird—the stopper of time."

"Octopus—the spiral of life."

"Frog—a water element."

"Butterfly—everlasting life."

"Wait. Butterfly, everlasting life," Boomer said excitedly, "that's the title of Salvador Collie's painting."

"What does it all mean?" Hindlick asked.

"Certainly, something to do with water." Roddy said.

"Not one of my favorite subjects," the bath-hating Boomer commented.

"Water and life, life and water," Roddy said. "Without water, our species would not survive."

"Without water, we wouldn't have to take a bath!" Boomer declared.

Roddy ignored Boomer's comment and once more reviewed the clues.

"The whale represents the power of water, life and death, and regeneration."

"What's regeneration?" Boomer asked,

"To be renewed, restored," Hindlick answered.

"To be spiritually reborn," Roddy added. He excitedly turned to the book and read. "The frog represents the elements of water. The hummingbird is the stopper of time. The octopus symbol is the spiral of life and the butterfly, everlasting life."

"All water and life symbols," Hindlick said.

Then, like a light suddenly being turned on, Roddy shouted out the answer to the life-and-death puzzle.

"The Fountain of Youth."

Chapter 26

The Fountain of Youth

As Roddy continued to flip through the pages of the mystical book, he marveled how ancient words magically turned into words that he could understand. It told the story of a land where there was a river, spring, or fountain where the waters had miraculous curative powers. Anyone who bathed in the waters would have all their ills cured and regain their youth.

Pounce de Leon, a famous explorer, learned of the fable from the natives. As described in the book, this body of water not only contained a spring of perpetual youth, but also teemed with gold and all sorts of riches. Pounce de Leon set out to find this land of riches and perhaps the mythical fountain that would restore his health and make him young again.

• • •

As he read through the book, Roddy was looking for further clues to better understand the motivation behind Dr. Dingo's bizarre behavior. Dingo was obviously angered at his treatment at the Arachnid Conference. His experiments with arachnids were brilliant, but they were met with scorn and ridicule from his peers. He sought revenge and used his brilliance, along with some undefined benefit from the moon, to turn the altered ticks into assassins. Roddy glanced over to the tick tanks and shuddered as he thought about the harm they could cause if ever released into the whole of Collywood society.

Roddy looked up from the book and said, "Salvador Collie probably found this book in a shop dealing with antiquities. Where Dr. Dingo found it is anyone's guess."

Dr. Hindlick added, "From what I understand, surrealistic artists, like Collie, were intrigued by fables like the *Fountain of Youth*; he playfully used his brush to paint the symbols into his paintings. Unfortunately for us, it seems we are in great danger because our demented doctor believes that the *Fountain of Youth* actually exists."

"I'm confused," Boomer said. "Dr. Dingo is no dummy. You don't think that he figured out the Fountain of Youth symbols like we did. So, what does he want from us?"

"Location, location, location" Ollie said in a surprisingly clear voice.

"How can we figure out the location of the *Fountain of Youth* if it doesn't actually exist?" Boomer asked.

"But in his mind it does exist," Roddy said. "and he's pretty desperate to find it. Dr. Hindlick, it's not hard to see that he's a pretty sick puppy."

Hindlick responded. "Obviously—Dr. Dingo walks with a cane. His foot definitely drags, and his coat is unusually dull. The hump on his back is an indication that the bones of the upper spine have collapsed, which can cause extreme pain."

"And his mental condition?" Roddy asked.

"How about bat-poop crazy?" Boomer said.

"I can't disagree with your colorful diagnosis, Boomer, He obviously has pronounced mood swings. One moment he's calm and composed, then suddenly he is completely consumed with rage. He's definitely manic. Dr. Dingo has serious health problems."

Roddy nodded agreement. "So he's frantically looking to kick-start his body parts and thinks finding the *Fountain of Youth* will do it."

"Mystery solved, we can all go home now?" Boomer whined.

Hindlick responded sympathetically. "I'm afraid not, Boomer. Unfortunately, the most important part of the mystery remains."

A dejected Boomer stared at the painting. "Ollie, is there something we missed? Can you see any other symbols in the painting that could tell us its location?"

Ollie's gaze shifted to the painting, but he could only shake his head 'no'. Dr. Hindlick once again took the metal name tag from his collar and jiggled it in Ollie's direction. Ollie easily fell back into a hypnotic trance, but it was obvious that he had nothing more to contribute. The realization that the captives had failed to find the final clue to Dingo's sadistic puzzle was devastating. They settled back in their cages and contemplated their fate.

Chapter 27

Failed Test

A chilling silence settled over the room. The captives lay exhausted in their cages, disheartened by their failure to solve the most important part of the mystery: the location of the *Fountain of Youth*. Even the ticks rested, perhaps in anticipation of being called upon to perform their final act of terror.

Roddy thought that the strange curative waters were probably nothing more than fable, but he continued to scan every inch of the canvas for a possible clue to its location. He was sure that the desperate Dr. Dingo would never accept that the restorative waters did not exist. He was intent on extending his life so that he could continue his work with the arachnids. Dingo was also obsessed with seeking revenge on Dr. Hindlick and the rest of Collywood's scientific community. Roddy had little doubt that his hatred was so deep that he wouldn't hesitate to turn his altered bloodsuckers loose on his captives, as well on the unsuspecting citizens of Collywood. He could not think rationally and reasoning was no longer an option. For one of the few times in his young life, Roddy felt helpless.

The stillness was interrupted by the tap, tap, tap of Dingo's cane. The doctor had returned. Tension hung over the room. Roddy saw hopelessness on the faces of the other caged prisoners. The tick buzz revved up again, softly at first, then increased when Dr. Dingo tapped his cane. He looked into the eyes of Dr. Hindlick and saw despair. His gaze then shifted to Roddy. Dr Dingo's sunken eyes seemed to pierce Roddy's soul. Roddy realized that Dr. Dingo was about to direct the tough question directly at him.

Why me? I'm still a pup. A very smart and brave pup, but still a pup.

Dr. Dingo's voice was strangely calm. "The answer to the question that I am about to ask will affect your lives. Think carefully before you answer."

Roddy felt tremendous apprehension. The crazed Dr. Dingo had put the fate of the entire Collywood community squarely on his shoulders. As he spoke, Dingo gestured toward the painting, "Do you and your friends understand the message that Salvador Collie conveyed in the painting?"

"I think so," Roddy said in a shaky voice.

"That's a good start. Do you care to share it with me?"

A shiver ran up his spine; he couldn't help but babble away. "There are hidden, like drawings in the painting, that say there is a river or lake or pool…

"Yes, yes…" Dingo drooled

"Or puddles [heh, heh] that can restore just about anything… even heartworm."

"And…" Dr. Dingo said excitably.

"The *Fountain of Youth,*" Roddy mumbled.

"Very good, my young friend." Roddy knew that coming up next would be the killer question.

"And did those symbols reveal the location of such waters?" The captives collectively held their breaths. Roddy waited a long moment and finally responded,

"Yes."

Dingo squealed with delight. Boomer, Ollie, and Hindlick were shocked.

"Where, where?" Dingo said with great anticipation.

Roddy took a deep breath, summoned up an inner-strength, and said using his most grown-up voice.

"Actually, it's not very far from here. I can take you there, but first you have to release the others."

Roddy watched as Dr. Dingo's sick mind mulled over his proposition. The expression on Dingo's face soon gave Roddy his answer. It turned from delight to disappointment and then finally to rage. He held his cane high in the air and screamed, "It's a trick to free your friends. Reveal the location to me now or I will release my horde of hungry ticks to feast on your blood."

Roddy changed tactics and went on the offensive. "There

is no *Fountain of Youth*. It's a legend started by an old fart who died hundreds of years ago, and Salvador Collie played it into a big hoax. He wanted a strong reaction to his painting and he sure got it."

"No! No! You're wrong!" Dingo screamed as he pointed to the leathery book. "It's all there in the book!"

Dr. Hindlick spoke in a kindly voice, "Dr. Dingo, I apologize for my conduct and for the way that my colleagues treated you at the Arachnid Conference. Your work was brilliant, and we were all jealous fools. I now see now how important it is for you to continue your work, but first we need to make you well. Unfortunately, the *Fountain of Youth* does not exist, but I can help. Allow me put you in the hospital for treatment."

At first, it appeared that Dr. Hindlick's reassuring words might have gotten through to Dr. Dingo. He stood before his captives, resting heavily on his cane. He seemed resigned that his dream for everlasting health was fading. Boomer looked at Roddy, hoping to get some acknowledgment that the nightmare was about to come to an end. Roddy stared back blankly. He had no idea how the next few moments would play out.

Then Dingo looked up slowly, and the expression on his face said everything. Dingo was a lunatic and a few reassuring words weren't about to change the years of hate and frustration that had consumed him.

"Without the waters, I will die," he said sadly. "Without the waters ... " The evil in his voice returned and he howled, "You, too, will die!" Dingo jammed the end of his cain against the button on the wall and the skylight slid open. The light from a full moon bathed the room, creating a tick frenzy. The captives were horrified to see the tick's overgrown bodies smash against the glass, desperately trying to free themselves.

Dr. Dingo screamed his orders. "Spew your venom into all who oppose us. Let them feel the pain that has consumed me these past years."

Dingo hobbled toward the cages, mumbling over and over again. "Feast, my friends, on all that oppose me."

When all seemed hopeless, Roddy once again pulled out his secret weapon and shot the Wandering Wand through the bars. It slashed wildly, whipped at Dingo's legs, and toppled him to the floor. He screamed out in pain, but continued to drag himself toward the glass tanks. Roddy raked Dr. Dingo with the wand, but an extraordinary burst of energy swept over the doctor's fragile body and drove him on, closer and closer to the tanks.

The captives could only watch in horror as Dr. Dingo raised his cane and, with a hideous cry, smashed it down on the tanks over and over again. The glass from the tanks splintered and split open. Hordes of screeching creatures tumbled out. The menacing, grotesque ticks with their overgrown bodies pulsed in anticipation of a blood feast.

To the captives, it looked like the gates of hell had burst open.

Chapter 28

Kick Tick Butt

The ticks hesitated a moment, waiting for Dr. Dingo's final command. Dingo rose slowly from the floor, his strength bolstered by the adrenalin rushing through his body. He smiled wickedly at his prisoners and, like a general urging on his troops, he extended his cane like a sword and signaled the ticks to press forward. Roddy's recurring nightmare was now reality, and this time it wasn't his mind playing tricks.

Boomer's stomach was churning. The fear of being devoured by a swarm of crazed ticks produced a noxious gas that circulated through his gut and soon BURST into the room.

Roddy's paw went up quickly to cover his nose, and he realized that Boomer had just let go the most toxic farts of his life. The ticks were stunned, their advancement slowed. A few retreated back toward their shattered tanks. Dr. Dingo, ignoring the fumes that circulated around the room, gagged out his orders.

"Attack! Attack!" The ticks were slow to react to Dingo's commands. Dingo raised his heavy cane and smashed it to the floor. Finally getting the attention of the ticks, Dingo urged his troops on.

"Focus, fearless arachnids." The captives realized that Boomer's blast of gas was but a temporary reprieve. They backed to the far ends of their cages in a futile effort to avoid the menacing ticks as they once again advanced. The sturdy bars that imprisoned them were no barrier to the menace heading their way. Roddy heard a few whimpers, but basically Dr. Hindlick, Boomer, and Ollie stood bravely in the face of certain death.

"You're toast, you ugly blood suckers!" Cujo's voice boomed above the screeching ticks.

Time seemed to stand still as Brittany and Cujo rappelled down through the skylight. The ticks froze, surprised by the sudden entrance of the bold pups.

"Kill them! Kill them!" Dr. Dingo barked before taking a swift karate kick from Brittany that sent him sprawling halfway across the room.

"Watch out, the tick's bite is poisonous!" Roddy shouted over the commotion.

"We're going to ice you suckers!" Cujo bellowed. As Cujo circled around the ticks, he tossed collars into the cages of the captives.

"Extra-strength tick repellent collars, fresh out of Whinestein's lab," he shouted over the commotion. Roddy and the others quickly strapped on the collars, then watched as Whinestein swung down from the opening in the roof. He held a hose in his paw that was attached to a canister strapped to his back.

Boomer, caught up in the excitement, yelled out encouragement to his friends, "Kick tick butt!"

"A little spray for the fray," Whinestein cried out triumphantly as a milky substance sprayed out of the hose, engulfing the confused ticks. The ticks scattered in panic. They tried desperately to retreat to their shattered glass tanks, but they never made it. They sprawled helplessly on their backs, trapped in Whinestein's deadly formula, their hairy legs, pointing toward the ceiling, quivering uncontrollably. Boomer and Ollie cheered wildly.

Cujo secured the dazed Dr. Dingo with a chain around his neck and searched his pockets. He held up a ring of keys and tossed them to Brittany, who promptly unlocked the cages and freed the happy captives.

With their last dying effort, a group of ticks turned on Dr. Dingo and swarmed over his prone body.

"Ooh…ooh…OOH!" the captives watched in shock as the case of 'Lunatick' came to a brutal ending.

There were high fours all around as the merriment continued. Brittany described how the pups went into action after

Roddy called about Boomer's disappearance. It didn't take long for the resourceful pups to discover Dr. Dingo's laboratory.

"Your timing is amazing," Boomer said, wiping his brow with his paw.

"Hey suckers, take that and that," Whinestein said, firing the last few squirts of his anti-tick concoction in the direction of the flailing insects. Brittany twirled her tick-repellent collar around in the air and the others joined in, howling and dancing around the dead ticks.

Chapter 29

The Press Conference

"Can you hear me? Is this thing on?" Mayor Corgi tapped the microphone. There was a murmur of approval from the crowd of city officials. A TV news crew from WOOF had their cameras trained on Mayor Corgi standing behind a lectern, displaying the *City of Collywood* emblem. Daily Barker reporters with notebooks in paws were scribbling notes and photographers were aiming their cameras at the podium. Standing next to Mayor Corgi, Captain Shepherd was looking very official in her dress uniform. Rod, Winnie, and Roddy were seated in the front row.

Mayor Corgi, who was running for a second term in office, had an inflated opinion of himself. He saw the press conference as a way to get positive television and newspaper coverage for his second-term run for mayor.

Germaine and Rod argued against having the press conference. There was a lot of recent activity at Collywood PD, with the high profile Petropolitan Museum case at the top of list. But truth be told, Collywood PD's involvement with the Petropolitan case was little more than mopping up afterwards. The real heroes who broke up Dr. Dingo's mad scheme had not been identified.

The microphone boomed out the deep voice of Mayor Corgi, "Good morning everyone. I'm proud to say that under my administration, crime in our city is at its lowest mark. I've worked closely with the brave officers at Collywood PD to protect our citizens from the bad dogs that, unfortunately still roam our streets."

Rod…*Dog-crap*

Germaine…*Dog-crap*

Reporters…*Dog-crap*

"Captain Shepherd, please step up and tell us about the latest exploits of your fine police department." As Germaine approached the lectern, the gathered group, eager to hear the substance of the press conference, applauded enthusiastically. Winnie jumped to her feet and shouted,

"Go girl!" Then slid back into her chair, a little embarrassed. Rod seemed annoyed, but Roddy gave her a paws up and whispered in her ear,

"Way to go, Mom."

As the mayor left the stage, Germaine shot Rod a look as if saying…*what in the devil should I say about the museum caper?*

Germaine took a deep breath, "Thank you, Mayor Corgi, for your kind words." Captain Shepherd put her notebook on the lectern, paused, and then said,

"Rod...Rod Weiler, would you please stand up?" Rod put his paws over his eyes and said to himself..._don't do this to me, Germaine._ Winnie poked Rod's shoulder and with the heavy applause from the group, Rod reluctantly stood up.

The captain continued, "Rod, you have a lot of fans out there. Can't think of a better partner in fighting crime." When the applause died down, Rod sat down.

"I'm proud to report that our brave officers of Collywood PD recently raided a warehouse on Turd Avenue, where they recovered a truck-full of illicitly gotten goods. When we cracked open the truck full of cartons, we found valuable, recently hijacked ..."

Roddy almost jumped out of his seat. Finally, he was about to find out about the reliability of the tip that he had left for his dad. _Great work dad,_ he thought, _for solving the mystery of the stolen art treasures from the New Yorkie's Guggenhound Museum._

"...SQUEAKY TOYS!"

Roddy almost fell off of his seat. _Squeaky toys? Not art treasures?_

Germaine pulled a squeaky toy out of her bag and held it up. "Brand new, latest technology with a new sounding squeak." Germaine squeezed the toy and its melodious tone set off a burst of applause and cheers.

"Thank you. Thank you." Germaine shouted over the clamor, as she moved away from the lectern.

A reporter shouted. "Wait, wait. What about the Petropolitan Museum case?" Germaine moved reluctantly back to the lectern.

"Oh, that," she said. "Okay…" Rod sat on the edge of his seat, wondering how the captain was going to spin the outcome of this mystery. "It started with the theft from the Petropolitan Museum of a valuable painting by Salvador Collie. Two guards, retired police dogs, were on duty."

"Scoop Trailer, Daily Barker," a reporter interrupted. "The guards—they got names?"

"Yes, I'm sorry. The name of the guards—Ollie McNally and Spike Spitz, a couple of ex police officers. The captain paused, then asked, "We have a lot to cover. Could you please hold your questions until the end? Thank you.

Germaine rushed through the details of the investigation.

The theft of the Salvador Collie's painting.

Spike's mind-altered assault on Ollie.

The transport of the painting to an accomplice at the emergency exit.

Dr. Dingo's weird experiment with ticks.

The anonymous call that led police to Dr. Dingo's secret lab.

The raid on the lab finding Ollie and Dr. Hindlick freed from their cages.

A room full of dead and dying ticks.

"Thanks to all our police officers…" Germaine was interrupted by the publicity-seeking lawyer, Flea Bailey, who jumped on the stage. He grabbed the microphone and berated Captain Shepherd and Rod Weiler. He blabbed away how Collywood PD had tormented his client, Al.K.Bone with actuations and intimidation. He threatened that a lawsuit would soon be filed. Despite the round of boos, Bailey stood smiling, next to Captain Shepherd as the cameras clicked away.

"Get that clown off of the stage." Was followed by other not-able-to-print comments. Bailey finally retreated into the crowd—but not before signing a few autographs.

A flustered Captain Shepherd was about to leave the stage, when *the* question was asked.

"Captain Shepherd, Wolf Bitzer, WOOF-TV. Are you saying that the police dogs arrived after…I repeat AFTER someone had already rescued the victims? How can you explain this?" Germaine shot a glance at Rod; took another deep breath, and related the story as told by Ollie and Dr. Hindlick.

"Oh, right! Both the doctor and Ollie told us that they were rescued by several…masked strangers, who repelled through the lab's skylight; subdued Dr. Dingo and used a strong insecticide to wipe out the ticks."

Since the pups had saved the lives of Dr. Hindlick and Ollie, they agreed not to make known the true identities of their rescuers.

So, we remain in the shadows. Roddy thought.

The reporters fired back with more questions.

"Who were those masked canines?"

Someone in the crowd shouted out,

"SUPER HEROES!

"Collywood has its own SUPER HEROES!"

● ● ●

"I'm proud of you, Dad," Roddy bravely hugged his dad. For the first time that he could remember, his dad hugged him back (and left some slobber on his head). After Roddy's harrowing nightmare, he knew that something had changed. He was growing out of puphood and realized that soon, the word 'pup' would no longer be used to describe him.

The hug from his dad was extremely meaningful. Roddy couldn't figure out the sudden show of affection. He thought for a moment…

"What the heck, I'll take it."

Chapter 30

The Cure All

Dr. Hindlick turned off the paved highway on to a dirt road that wound its way to the top of Collywood Hills. The headlights of Hindlick's Land Rover cut through the darkness, revealing heavy brush that closed in on the narrowing road. Overgrown branches from the bushes scraped against the sides of the Land Rover as it slowly pushed on through the moonlit night. Heavy rains over the years had pockmarked the road. Each time a tire found a hole, Dr. Hindlick winced in pain. His limbs were growing numb, the pain in his side was more intense, and his vision was failing.

A single venom-laden tick had freed itself from Whinestein's milky muck and found Hindlick's cage. In a final burst of fury, the tick's sharp fang had punctured the doctor's leg and injected a fatal dose of venom. It took a few days before Dr. Hindlick realized the extent of the infection inflicted by the tick, and by then it was too late. He was dying, and there was no antidote that could save him.

After the rescue, Dr. Hindlick was seen multiple times at the museum, standing for hours studying the Salvador's Collie's *Everlasting* painting. Little did anyone know that it wasn't just his admiration of the painting, but rather a matter of life-or-death. In his delirium, he pictured every inch of Salvador Collie's painting clearly in his mind: every brush stroke, every shape, and every symbol.

The Land Rover pushed on until the road ended in heavy brush. Hindlick pushed open the door and fell to the road. He rested for a moment and then, calling on every ounce of strength left in his ravished body, he half-walked, half-crawled through the thickening brush. He stumbled over rotting tree trunks that littered the ground and fell into a patch of thorny branches that tore at his body, opening new wounds.

"Just a little further," he whimpered. "Give me strength." He knew his time was running out, and prayed that the next moment would bring him to his destination. With the last steps that he could muster, he broke through the brush. His vision was almost gone, so he couldn't see the moonlight as it peered out from behind a cloud and danced on the surface of the lake. He heard the soothing ripple of the water and the serenading insects that skipped along its surface. He took one last breath, and tumbled into the cool water.

He floated aimlessly, face down in the crystal clear water, too weak to lift his head above the surface. The last breath of air was just leaving his lungs when suddenly he found a spurt of energy and rolled on to his back. His body hung effortlessly on the surface. A strange tingling feeling started at the tips of his paws and then raced quickly through his body. Life returned to his limbs. He splashed joyously. He took a huge breath of the night air that filled every corner of his lungs. His long exhale seemed to expel everything that was damaging his body. He suddenly felt strong and strangely youthful. Dr. Hindlick looked up to the starry sky and imagined that the face in the moon was smiling at him.

Epilogue

Roddy leaned against his doghouse—his eyes fixed on the Collywood Hills rising in the distance.

"SUPER HEROES? Got a nice ring to it."

PREVIEW

BOOK 2

In MY FATHER IS A POLICE DOG Series

Chapter 1

Visitors from Pluto

The sky sparkled above the huge dome of the famous Collywood Planetarium. Professor Cosmo Dane lifted his glasses to his forehead and gazed through the eyepiece of a giant telescope. He slowly turned a few knobs that adjusted a series of delicately polished lenses, marveling how such a slight touch of his paw could bring into view solar systems that were millions of light years away.

Professor Dane was the foremost expert in the science of the origin and development of the universe. As a highly respected professor of Astronomy and Cosmology, he had devoted his life to the study and explanation of the nature of the universe. He was considered by Space scientists as the foremost scholar in space exploration and the study of natural phenomena in outer space. His awards were numerous. His life's dream became reality when, several years earlier, he was awarded the prestigious Puplizer Prize for his extensive work on the origins of Pluto.

Cosmo Dane had been a strong advocate for the existence of life in the universe, other than on his own small planet. Any unusual disturbances out in the vastness of space got his attention.

Suddenly, a large cylindrical shape cut across his vision. Cosmo jumped back, rubbing his eyes in disbelief. He held his breath, then once again peered through the telescope. This time he saw only the brilliance of the sparkling night sky.

With a big exhale the professor said to himself, *Been working too hard.* He was convinced that his mind was playing tricks.

Professor Dane studied a group of astral charts that covered the surface of a large table. He took out a small notebook from the pocket of his lab jacket and made a few notations. Then, once again, he looked through the eyepiece of the huge telescope that shot up majestically from the dome of the planetarium. He chuckled as he thought about what appeared to be an image of a spaceship passing across the eye of his telescope.

"Guess the next thing I'll see are furry little creatures from Pluto running around Collywood." With his face pressed tightly against the eye-piece of the huge telescope, he failed to notice the bizarre activity happening just outside of the large windows of the planetarium.

Eerie, glowing forms fell from the sky, floating down like iridescent snowflakes.

<To be continued>

Authors Note

The signs have been there. It's not like we haven't had our suspicions: the intelligence behind their expressive eyes, the subtle tilt of their head, the way that their ears perk up like antenna and track our conversations. Either dogs have a freaky chip in their brain that translates our language into canine, or they've learned how to read our lips. The point is, they understand us very well. So, if they can hear us, can they speak? Well, we know they can speak, but can they *talk*? We acknowledge that dogs communicate by barking, growling, and whimpering. We can't hear what they're actually saying, but, then again, we can't hear a dog whistle either.

About the Author

DL Rosenblit started his career writing for children's TV shows and freelancing as a comedy writer. As a Creative Director for an advertising agency, he wrote commercials for kid-focused accounts including several toy companies and McDonalds restaurants. A dog food commercial he wrote early in his career was the inspiration for several screenplays introducing the world of Collywood, starring dog detective, Rod Weiler. The LUNATICK introduces middle grade readers to Rod and his crime-busting son, Roddy Weiler, and is the author's first in the MY FATHER IS A POLICE DOG mystery series.

Made in the USA
Monee, IL
15 January 2021